The Hounded Heart

THE HOUNDED HEART

♥

ESTELLA WOLD

AVALON BOOKS
THOMAS BOUREGY AND COMPANY, INC.
401 LAFAYETTE STREET
NEW YORK, NEW YORK 10003

PRINTED IN THE UNITED STATES OF AMERICA
ON ACID-FREE PAPER
BY HADDON CRAFTSMEN, SCRANTON, PENNSYLVANIA

Thanks to John and his Irish wolfhounds, to Bunny,
and to past and present North Coast Writers.

Special thanks to my writing partners for this story:
fellow Avalon writers Alice Sharpe and C. Dell Turney.

Chapter One

Beth slowed for another hairpin curve. The road cut through the redwood forest like a stream winding through a deep canyon. So little light sifted through the giant trees that Beth nearly missed the road sign she had been watching for. *Scenic Loop,* it proclaimed, *500 Feet.*

Beth's stomach shivered around a lump of ice. It was nearly sunset. The daylong drive from San Francisco had tired her. Yet now she was willing to retrace every mile rather than face what waited for her down that turn-off.

Think of Jenny, she told herself. *You have to do this for her.*

She took a deep breath. She could scarcely believe she was retracing the route her own mother had used thirty years ago to flee from the family home. By the time Beth signaled for the turn, her hands were shaking. *There's nothing to be afraid of. If things don't work out, just stick to business—and beat a swift retreat.*

This road was narrower than the highway she had left. Only a few ferns reached enough sunlight to flourish along the roadside. Beyond them stretched a dead wasteland of fallen redwood twigs that had dried to the color of old pennies. Through this redwood duff, a fallen limb reached up to splay its bare branches into the air.

The limb looked like the forearm of a monster from her childhood nightmares, a beast that clawed through the ground groping for its victims. Sometimes Beth would escape by waking. More often, the monster's glowering red eyes found her, and its claws pulled her underground to bury her alive.

Fifty feet ahead there suddenly appeared a red light. It glowered like those eyes from her childhood nightmares. Beth gasped, then chided herself. *Don't be silly! It's only a road flare!*

She slowed down. Around the bend another flare appeared. *I wouldn't be this jumpy if I weren't so nervous about coming here under a false identity!*

She applied the brakes cautiously and slowed to a stop. She wasn't used to driving much, and this was the first time she had ever driven her boss's car. In San Francisco she rode to work on a clanging cable car. The money she saved from not owning a car went into her "Jenny Fund."

More red lights flashed ahead, where a station wagon and a Jeep lay end to end across the road, the station wagon's front bumper crumpled against the base of an enormous tree. A third vehicle, a forest ranger's pickup, blinked its warning lights. The road was completely blocked.

Beth hoped the absence of an ambulance meant that no one was hurt. Certainly, no one was moving with the serious urgency that would have indicated a medical crisis. She sighed and rolled down her window. In the distance she heard a woman sobbing. It looked like a long wait.

A squat man wearing a ranger's uniform approached Beth's car.

"Was anyone hurt?" Beth asked him.

"Just shaken up. Clearing the road for traffic is the problem now." Someone hailed him from the wreckage. "Over here!" the ranger hollered back, and two more men headed Beth's way and joined him. One man was rubbing his elbow. His taller companion was keeping an eye on him.

"You should turn around while you can," the ranger told Beth. "Scenic driving along this stretch of the road is over for an hour or so."

"But I'm turning off just beyond here!"

"You must have your directions wrong, miss. There's only one place in the next ten miles, and the Malverns don't cotton much to sightseers. You'll have to turn back before another car comes up behind you and blocks your escape."

Beth's mind raced. *Escape? Not when I'm this close to following things through!* She gripped the steering wheel tightly. "I can't turn back now! It's a family matter!"

Those words had slipped out before she realized it— *a family matter.*

The three men stared at her. The tall newcomer bent over to peer through the windshield. Beth saw that his dark, loose curls came close to needing a haircut. But it was his eyes, the color of steel, that suddenly riveted her to her seat. His gaze felt strong enough to break through her barriers and read all her secrets.

Just then a large woman limped up. A gauze bandage covered the broad expanse of her upper arm. "Could you check it again?" she whimpered to the tall man.

The gray eyes turned to the bandage and freed Beth.

Stay calm, Beth told herself. *He's just a nosy medic.*

The shorter man slapped the ranger on the shoulder. "I think I can squirrel my Jeep outta there if Mrs. Laurence doesn't mind her bumper taking a scratch or two."

The woman shrugged her good shoulder.

The ranger gave him the go-ahead, then turned back to Beth. "Maybe it won't be such a long wait, after all. That is, if you're sure you have business at the Malvern place."

"Yes!" Beth too quickly agreed. "I have business there." The unsettling gray eyes found her again. She concentrated on the retreating figure of the Jeep's owner and tried to sound more official. "They've hired me to work with a problem dog."

The large woman came alive. "*That's* what ran me off the road! It was one of the Malverns' monster dogs!"

"Now, Polly," the ranger began, "first you said it was a cougar; now it's a giant dog. If you ask me, it was a deer. You've lived here long enough to know you have to slow down this time of day, when the deer head for water."

"It was one of those huge beasts of the Malverns'," the woman cried. "Big as a deer. Sort of tannish—"

"Deer colored?" the ranger asked.

"Yes, deer colored—" She stopped, then flushed bright pink. "N-no! Not quite *that* color!"

The ranger chuckled.

"It's not funny!" the woman grumbled.

The Jeep grunted to life, then shifted back and forth against the tree and the station wagon hemming it in. All at once it cleared the redwood and broke free.

The ranger motioned to Beth. "You go ahead now, miss."

"It's not funny!" the woman echoed.

Beth started the engine. The tall man looked her way again, but she was determined not to give those eyes of steel anything further to pry loose.

As Beth inched past her, the bandaged woman shook a fist at the car. "And you won't think it's funny, either, lady. Not when one of those hellhounds turns on you!"

Beth bit her lip as she left the accident site behind her. *Nice going, genius! Nearly slipping up like that! All anyone needs to know is the part about coming to train an eccentric old lady's dog. That way the rest of it can be forgotten . . . if things don't work out.*

Beth didn't want to think about things not working out. That meant returning to San Francisco for more of the same—constant worry about her older sister Jenny, Beth's ward since their mother's death.

Though they lived together, Jenny required supervision when Beth was at work. State programs took care of Jenny's basic needs, but Beth wanted more for her sister than the basics. The specialists might be right about Jenny never leaving her strange, private world of autism—but Beth was determined to make that world as bright as possible.

When the odometer showed Beth she had traveled three miles since leaving the highway, she looked for and found a driveway branching to the left. It was barely sunset, yet the narrow lane seemed as dark as midnight—and just as cold. She flicked on the headlights. Ahead in the tall ferns, the lights caught and held two fiery points. They vanished just as Beth realized they were eyes.

Despite the Deer Crossing signs she'd seen for miles,

she felt these eyes belonged to a predator. The woman at the accident had mentioned a cougar. Though she knew dogs well, Beth felt ignorant about wild animals. *Never mind,* she told herself. *This car is as safe as an armored tank.*

The written directions to the house had warned her the driveway was a long one. *A thousand miles long would be fine with me,* Beth thought, remembering the people she would soon face, people from whom she must hide her true identity.

She drew a hurried breath. For the fiftieth time that day, she coached herself on her new name. *Eliza Elliott, Eliza Elliott, Eliza Elliott.*

The Eliza part was easy to live with. Her name truly was Elizabeth, though no one had ever called her that but a strict fourth-grade teacher who hated nicknames. Beth had assured herself she was merely using part of her full name.

The Elliott part was harder to justify. When her boss offered to lend her his car, she got the idea to borrow his last name too. So Beth Orne had turned herself into Eliza Elliott in all correspondence between the dog-obedience program she managed and Rebecca Malvern, whose home was somewhere ahead through the maze of tree trunks and darkness the driveway had become.

Rebecca Malvern . . . my grandmother! Beth swallowed hard. She didn't want to think of everything that entailed. *Not now, not yet.*

A light winked through the trees. Beth was so intent on gauging the light's distance that she almost missed noticing what barred the driveway. She braked in time to avoid hitting a sawhorse set dead in the middle of the lane.

She considered her options. She could move the sawhorse and drive on, or she could park and go the remaining distance on foot. The household expected her to arrive after dark, so perhaps the barrier was intended to warn her of a road hazard ahead. She remembered the eyes at the base of the driveway. A chill shot through her.

Reason took over. She doubted she truly had seen a cougar. But even if she had, an animal with such a reputation for aloofness surely wouldn't venture this near the house and grounds of humans.

Maybe she imagined the eyes. Maybe they belonged to that boogeyman from her childhood nightmare. And maybe if she had remembered to stop for lunch, she wouldn't be feeling so light-headed and jumpy now.

Maybe, maybe, maybe. One thing she knew for certain—she wasn't about to sit there all night. Indecision wouldn't help her credibility as the trainer of the giant-dog breeds. Resolutely she dug through her shoulder bag and found the tiny flashlight she always carried but never seemed to use. Finally it would justify those months she had packed it along.

She stepped into the damp, cool air, feeling alarmingly vulnerable in the thin summer clothes that conducted the chill right to her instead of protecting her from it. Her warm wraps were inside her suitcase, locked in the trunk. *So much for the armored tank.*

A grove of redwood trees towered over her, still and watchful. One by one, stars filled the sky. Beth shivered and decided to dig out a sweater. When she flicked on the flashlight, however, a sickly yellow beam wavered over the road ahead. She decided to go without the sweater. The flashlight batteries didn't have much life left in them. *Better hurry,* she told herself, *before they die!*

She hadn't gone far when she first heard something.

At first she thought it was only falling leaves, so subtle was the sound. Then she remembered it was late August and she was in an evergreen forest. The sound grew closer, developing into a distinct rhythm. A pattering.

She hurried on. For one moment she was certain she had left the sound behind. But then it started up again, faintly, insidiously, first to her right, then to her left.

Dim light filtered through the trees ahead. Beth made out the silhouette of a huge house. She moved from a walk to a jog. The sound behind her increased in tempo to match her quickened pace. Now it separated into two sources that came on faster and faster, closing in on her.

The driveway curved sharply away from the house lights. Leaving the lane, Beth aimed herself through the stand of trees separating her from the house. The flashlight did not shine far enough ahead to help.

She ran now, her hands outstretched, her feet sinking into deep drifts of redwood duff and stumbling over roots, her face swiped and slapped by low branches. Through it all, she kept aiming herself at the lights.

The faster she pushed herself, the closer came the sounds, now growing into the muffled padding of large paws. She thought again of cougars and felt the terror of a deer being pursued.

No sooner had she acknowledged the terror than it began to weigh her down. Her chest tightened into a knot. Breathing became gasping.

She seemed to get no closer to her destination. Always

a new clump of giant trees separated her from the lights. Now, from the direction of the house, she heard fragments of music—faint drawn-out notes from a single instrument.

A nearby sound, low and guttural, startled her. She gasped and spun away from it. In the darkness she lost her bearings and then her balance. She stumbled to one knee. From the other side a huge darkness bore down on her.

She struggled to stand up. For a fraction of a second the outline of an enormous head loomed over her, silhouetted against the starlight. Rearing several feet above her, the creature seemed caught in a web of darkness.

Suddenly it bore down on her. Hot breath flooded her cheek and neck. Something heavy pressed on each shoulder. A massive weight forced her backward, pushing her to the ground.

Beth went limp. *Play dead! Don't panic,* she told herself.

Years of training took over. The hot breath, the creature's smell—it was all too familiar. Dog.

She concentrated on steadying her voice. It must communicate control. Of the basic commands, the one for this situation was an all-purpose "Down." Some trainers developed an "Off" or "Back." If this dog didn't understand those, however, Beth would begin on a note of failure that might undermine her switching to "Down." She decided to play it safe and start with "Down." She hoped the giant pinning her to her back wouldn't take that as an order to sit on her. From the pressure exerted by his paws alone, she estimated his weight to be around one hundred and seventy pounds. "Down!"

The heavy paws at her shoulders twitched slightly. *"Down!"*

One paw lifted, then the other. She was free. She stood slowly and held still while her attacker and his companion sniffed her over. Beth was in known territory now and feeling silly for her earlier reaction. It was too dark to see him, but she could tell her attacker's nose reached up to her elbow. The second dog's nose rose even higher.

Beth could also tell the dogs were calming down and expressing simple curiosity. She was willing to give them all the time they needed to convince themselves she was no threat. The household had several wolfhounds besides the one she was to retrain, yet something wasn't right. Since the family was expecting her tonight, why would they block the road and let two giant dogs roam the grounds?

Something else was odd. In ancient days Irish wolfhounds worked in pairs, chasing a single wolf for miles. Once they ran it down, each dog grabbed an ear or cheek and held tight until the master arrived to finish the job. Gentle dogs, they used their teeth for restraining enemies, not for tearing them apart. Yet her attacker had used *paws* rather than teeth. That wasn't wolfhound behavior.

She was squinting at his dark shape, trying to make out its contours, when the second dog touched her. A warm tongue gave her hand a tentative lick.

"Hello, fella," she said. Her fingers sought that dog's head. They found wiry, inch-long hair at the crown, then stroked a slender muzzle—a wolfhound's, for sure. She guessed the dog stood over three feet tall at the shoulders. Held high, his head added another nine inches. Confident she had made one friend, Beth reached for the dog that had knocked her down. She barely had time to discover its hair was smooth and short before the dog shied from her touch.

Beth retrieved her flashlight. It had grown dimmer than a glowworm. She turned it off, pocketed it, then groped for the wolfhound's collar. She couldn't give him the "Heel" order, because then he would expect her to lead the way. She considered her options. Wolfhounds were a type of sight hound, dogs with keener eyes than other breeds.

She patted the dog's tall back. "Let's see if those superior eyes can keep us from walking into trees."

They had gone ten feet or so when the wolfhound stopped abruptly and tensed. Beth could hear the sound of a car's motor winding its way up the drive. Soon it would have to stop where her borrowed car blocked the way. Beth heard the free dog break into a run and head toward the car. Clearly the dogs weren't dangerous, but an unsuspecting frail or older person could be knocked down and hurt.

"Come!" she hollered, but the mystery dog did not obey.

The wolfhound strained to follow his companion yet respected Beth's tug on his collar. He whimpered slightly.

"Oh," she said, ruffling his ears, "you big fellas are such babies when you don't get your way."

Brakes squealed. Two blasts of a horn tore the air.

A breeze started up. Beth pulled closer to the wolfhound, glad for the warmth radiating from his body. She waited. Once the engine stopped and the car door opened, she would holler, warning the driver to stay in the car.

The engine had no sooner died, however, than a deep voice spoke. "Saxon! Who let you out? You rascal—"

The breeze picked up, stirring the treetops to a loud rushing sound that drowned out the rest of what the man was saying. Beth knew it would be futile to shout over the sound of the wind in the trees. Besides, the newcomer was in little danger if he knew the mystery dog by name.

Suddenly lights flooded the area ahead, silhouetting the trees that remained in Beth's path. She urged the wolfhound forward. After skirting two clumps of trees, they stepped from black forest into a semicircle of brightness. Floodlights lit up an enormous house. Stairs led to a vast porch where a figure stood in an open doorway.

"Hello!" Beth called from thirty feet away. When no one answered, she tried again. "I have your dog."

The figure moved into the light and resolved itself into a middle-aged woman. Light shone through the woman's puffy hairdo, turning it into a giant spider that clutched her skull. She fiddled with something hung around her neck.

The wolfhound tried to slink behind Beth. "You big baby," she whispered, then added more forcefully, "Heel!"

The giant dog reluctantly took his place and moved in unison with her toward the house.

"Who's out there?" the woman on the porch demanded.

"B—" Beth caught herself in time. "Eliza Elliott. I believe you were expecting me."

"Oh!" the woman said. She turned toward the door. "Irma! Ir-ma! Someone's here!"

Beth let the wolfhound go as they reached the steps. He started to follow her, then whimpered and stopped.

The woman on the porch shrank dramatically back into the doorway. "Keep him away!"

Beth turned toward the dog. In the light she could make out his color, a muted brindle in shades of gray. He had lain down, his head flat on the ground, a huge paw to each side of it. Two sorrowful eyes peered up at her. He looked like a timid puppy not sure what to do with himself.

"Well," Beth said, "he befriended me easily enough."

"Don't trust any of them!" the woman quavered. Petite and in her late fifties, she weighed half as much as the huge dog. No longer backlit, her hairdo had lost its sinister look and now simply glinted with dried hairspray maintaining a veneer of orderliness over the teased strands.

Another woman appeared. Tall, solid as a fireplug, her hair circled her crown in a simple gray plait.

"Irma," the first woman said, "this is Miss Elliott."

Beth climbed the stairs. "Please call me . . . Eliza."

Irma wiped her hands on a white towel. "Then you're the one who's come to train Mrs. M's dog?"

Beth nodded and offered her hand. Irma shook it.

The first woman frowned. "I'm Louisa Carstairs," she said. "*Mrs.* Carstairs. And this is our *housekeeper,* Irma Smythe." The thrust of her chin and tone of her voice indicated her disapproval of Beth's friendly gesture toward the hired help. Yet she did not offer her own hand. "Forgive me for not introducing myself at once," she continued, "but you startled me—the way you reached the house so quickly from your car. I'll make sure your room is ready." She thrust her chin up again and scurried off.

Beth stared at the housekeeper in bewilderment. "Oh!" she said. "She must think I'm the one who honked the horn. But I'm not. There's a second car. Someone who knows the other dog by name. 'Saxon,' he called it."

The housekeeper smiled. "That'll be our Ross back from his call. Come in, come in. Night turns damp quickly here. My husband has a fresh pot of coffee on, and we were about to have a snack. You can join us— if you don't mind kitchen folk, that is." She ended with a thrust of the chin clearly meant to mimic Louisa Carstairs's parting gesture.

"A snack sounds wonderful," Beth said. "I skipped lunch." Before she could enter the house, she heard the plaintive whimper of the big dog. "And him?" she asked.

"He's welcome in my kitchen," Irma said, "regardless of what some others may think of him. Come on, you big scamp."

But the wolfhound was paying them no heed. He rose. His long tail up in a graceful curve, he peered down the drive into the darkness. Then he trotted in that direction when two figures broke into the light. One, a dog's, loped forward to greet the wolfhound. Fawn-colored and inches shorter than the wolfhound, this dog was much heavier in build. Deep folds of skin around the eyes and mouth gave his huge head an air of grave and worried introspection.

"Oh!" Beth laughed. "A mastiff! That explains the paws—and the shyness." As she walked down the stairs, she made the mistake of looking into a floodlight. She lowered herself to a relaxed crouch, hands outstretched, palms up. Temporarily blinded, she heard the wolfhound circling back to her as if to show his aloof friend that Beth could be trusted. Wolfhounds were often shy with strangers. In Beth's experience, mastiffs were even more so.

Dark spots floated before her eyes. "Hey, fella," Beth called in the soft drawl that always worked best for her with shy dogs. "Don't you want to give me another hug?"

From the blur ahead of her came the sound of someone clearing his throat. "Another one?" a deep male voice began. "I'm afraid I don't recall any previous hugs."

After a stunned moment Beth could feel herself blushing. Did he think she was speaking to him? Rising, she addressed the blurred figure. "I—I didn't see you."

"Then we're even," he said lightly. "I nearly didn't see your car blocking the drive."

He was still a mysterious swarm of dark spots before Beth's eyes. Because she couldn't read his expression, she felt at a disadvantage. "A sawhorse blocked the drive," she said crisply. "My car stopped inches from it."

"So you decided to walk the rest of the way?"

"Well . . . yes," she faltered. *Is he challenging my story? Or am I just expecting people to challenge it?*

"This is that dog trainer Mrs. M sent for," Irma said.

Beth heard the man's sudden intake of breath. Her eyes were beginning to recover from the shock of the floodlight. Already she could make out more of his outline. He stood over six feet, nearly six inches taller than she.

"Come on, the both of you," Irma continued. "Ross, can't you see Eliza's ready to catch her death?"

Beth shivered. She didn't like the sound of that.

"Eliza?" he asked, something in his voice relaxing.

Beth was tired of questions. "Eliza Elliott. I'm here to work with a wolfhound. If you'd like, I could spare some time for your mastiff. A shy dog is a dangerous one when cornered." She hoped that sounded professional.

"I'll move the cars," he said. "May I have your keys?"

He definitely sounded more friendly now, but Beth still felt wary. "Thanks, but I'll take care of it." She walked up the stairs to Irma. "May I borrow a flashlight?"

Irma took Beth by the arm. "I'll send my son with Ross after the cars. Come warm up with that cup of coffee I promised. You must be exhausted after that long drive!"

Beth turned over her keys to Irma and let her lead her into the wide foyer. She knew the housekeeper was right—the daylong drive had tired her out. Besides, she didn't know if she could keep up her guard much longer, and the blurred stranger made her feel she had to do just that.

She scarcely noticed her surroundings until Irma led her down a long, dim hall. Her vision was nearly back to normal. She drew a sharp breath. *Mom grew up here.*

No sooner had that thought crossed her mind than she stepped into a bright kitchen. At the table sat a man and a teenaged boy. The man looked like a weathered version of the tall boy in the letterman's jacket. Irma introduced Beth to her husband and son, then sent her son, Arnie, to move Beth's car and fetch her luggage.

Beth accepted a steaming mug of coffee. She cupped her hands around it and drew its warmth into her chilled fingers. The brindle wolfhound settled on the floor behind the table and assumed the position of a shaggy, comical sphinx. His dark-amber eyes watched Beth expectantly.

Irma brought the dog meat scraps, which he sniffed with typical wolfhound caution before he ate them. Then she passed Beth a plate of cheese sandwiches and filled in her husband, Frank, on Beth's arrival.

"Sawhorse?" Frank looked perplexed. "Sometimes Arnie blocks the drive when we've got water hoses running across it. No reason for him to use a sawhorse that far from the house, though."

"Well," Irma said, "it's a good thing Eliza knows her way around big dogs. Nothing to pin on them this time."

Beth caught the knowing look that passed between husband and wife. "I need some information," she began, "about the dog I'm to work with. Mrs. Malvern only wrote that she broke her hip and couldn't continue his training."

Frank cocked his head. "You mean you don't know about Mrs. M's accident?"

Just then Louisa Carstairs returned. She was breathing rapidly, her cheeks nearly as pink as her blouse. Her hairdo looked disheveled. "Accident, indeed!" she cried. "It was a vicious attack!"

"Mrs. M says it was an accident," Irma countered.

Louisa's chin jerked up. "No one seems to remember that my husband and daughter witnessed it. That beastly dog charged Mother and knocked her down the stairs. If I'd had my way, he would have been immediately destroyed!" Just then she noticed the wolfhound. She stepped backward dramatically. "Who let that brute in here?"

"Mrs. M lets her dogs roam freely," Frank said.

Louisa glared at him. "Well, Mother is in no condition to decide such matters these days. I'm in charge now."

"There's something in your hair," Irma said.

Louisa found and disentangled a small twig. Her face flushed darker. "I must have brushed against the curtain in our guest's bedroom just now when I closed the window. How many times have I told you to clean more thoroughly, Irma?" With that she spun on her heels and marched out of the room.

Beth sat stunned until her hand began shaking so hard she spilled hot coffee down her fingers. *She called Rebecca Malvern "Mother." That makes Louisa Carstairs . . . my aunt!*

Chapter Two

Beth lay on her back, staring at the ceiling of the bedroom assigned her. Irma Smythe had spirited her there after announcing, "You look all dragged out." A cool breeze slipping through the window stirred the airy white curtains.

Beth's emotions raced along a roller-coaster track. One minute she felt charged with purpose: *Jenny—this is for her sake.* The next moment found her plummeting toward despair. *Louisa Carstairs for a sister? No wonder Mom ran away!*

As a child, Beth had sometimes asked why her relatives all came from her father's side of the family. Her mother always looked so sad that one day Beth's father took her aside and told her not to bring the subject up again.

"We'll talk about it when you're a little older," he assured her. His wife's senior by eighteen years, Phillip Orne put too many hours of overtime into his veterinarian practice. He died before he could keep his promise to Beth.

For a while grief pushed the topic from Beth's mind. By the time her curiosity resurfaced, she had matured enough not to want to renew a subject so painful to her mother. Beth had one clue to go on—her mother's family had raised and bred Irish wolfhounds, the tallest of all

19

dogs. Beth's own family kept a wolfhound until Phillip Orne's death forced them to economize. They moved into an apartment with no room for dogs. Sadly they turned over their wolfhound to Phillip Orne's former partner. To give Beth a chance to visit the dog regularly, the kindly vet hired her to do odd jobs around his home and clinic after school.

Beth soon acquired a reputation for understanding and effectively dealing with difficult dogs. After graduation she studied with a famous trainer and worked for a business specializing in training problem dogs. Eventually her boss named her manager of a new branch of Barking Up the Wrong Tree. Wolfhounds were less likely to develop serious behavior problems than most dogs, so opportunities seldom arose for Beth to work with them. Still, she always jumped at the chance to do so. Not only did she love the breed, but she also knew that Irish wolfhounds were a link to the mysterious side of her heritage and to her mother's past.

It was only after her mother's sudden death from a stroke that Beth discovered anything further about that side of her family. Tackling the sad task of going through her mother's papers, she came across her parents' faded marriage license. From it she learned two facts. First, that the civil ceremony had been performed nearly three hundred miles north of San Francisco, in the California town of Eureka. Second, that her mother's maiden name was Malvern.

Malvern—the name had struck Beth as vaguely familiar. She wondered if it could be connected to the only other fact she knew about her mother's childhood—Irish wolfhounds. Sure enough, a check through AKC registrations of that breed turned up the name of a Rebecca Malvern. Until twenty years ago, Malvern Kennels had turned out champion wolfhounds. Then, however, the kennels stopped showing their dogs. Records showed that the owner, Rebecca Malvern, lived in a remote part of northwestern California. Beth located the area on a map and discovered it was in the same county as the one in which her parents had married.

Exhaustive sleuthing through state and county records yielded more information. Beth found George and Rebecca Malvern who were parents of two children, a Rebecca L. Malvern and a younger daughter whose name and birth date confirmed her as Beth and Jenny's mother, Helen. Further digging brought sadder news. George Malvern had died within a few years of Helen's birth. That left Beth and Jenny with a grandmother and an aunt, both named Rebecca.

Beth had wondered how to contact them. For weeks she agonized over a letter to her grandmother. She tore up draft after draft. In the end, she sent a note, briefly identifying herself and informing Rebecca Malvern that her daughter Helen had died. Beth mentioned her sister but decided to say nothing yet about Jenny's disability. Experience had taught her how difficult it was to explain autism to those who had never lived with it.

She mailed the note. Weeks passed, then months, as Beth's hopes faded. She never heard from her grandmother.

But Lewis Elliott, owner of Barking Up the Wrong Tree, did. For Lewis, it was just a routine request for help with a problem dog. When he learned that the dog was a large one, he phoned the branch of his business that Beth managed.

"I know how you love wolfhounds," he had told her, "but this one may not be for you. For one thing, the owner wants someone immediately. I told her that my best trainer was about to go on vacation and wouldn't be taking on new clients until she got back. That woman's an insistent old bird, though. She demands that my best trainer take a paid vacation at her place! It seems that she refuses to ship the dog away from home. Can you believe that?"

Beth sighed. "This looks like the first wolfhound I've ever had to pass up. Unless the woman lives in Bermuda or Tahiti, I'm not giving up my vacation—even though Jenny and I are only staying home again this year."

"No such luck," Lewis said. "She's only a day's drive north of us, somewhere up in Humboldt County."

Beth jerked to attention. "Wh-what is her name?"

"Rebecca Malvern."

Beth dropped the receiver. A moment passed before she realized it was squawking at her from the floor. She retrieved the phone. Before she knew it, she had blurted out the whole story to Lewis.

"It sounds like you need to go up there, Beth."

"After she wouldn't even answer my letter? I don't know. Besides, why does she need a trainer from this area?"

"That's what I asked her," Lewis said. "It turns out she considers herself to be the only qualified trainer in her neck of the woods. But she's broken her hip and can't get to work on the problem her dog has just developed. Yet she wants it corrected before it takes root in his behavior pattern. That's certainly understandable."

Beth's thoughts wandered. "Even though she ignored my letter, I keep thinking that if she only understood our situation, she might be willing to help out with Jenny."

"If she's well off enough to bring a trainer to her dog, she can certainly afford to help her own flesh and blood!" Lewis's tone softened. "You're too young to deny yourself the good things in life because of Jenny."

Beth took a deep breath. She had had this argument often with Lewis and his wife since the three of them had become close friends. "I know you mean well, Lewis. I can only repeat that Jenny has special needs, special expenses. I'm all she has now." Then she brightened. "Oh, Lewis! If I take this job, I can afford to send Jenny to a special camp for developmentally disabled adults while I'm gone!"

Lewis asked if her grandmother knew that Beth was connected to Barking Up the Wrong Tree.

"I didn't mention anything in my letter about my line of work. Could her phone call just be a coincidence?"

"Anyone who has a problem giant dog and wants the best trainer is bound to find us," Lewis said. "Every wolfhound breeder on the Coast knows our record—*your* record, I should say. Most of them ask for you by name."

Beth swallowed hard. "Did she?"

"No. When she called, she only said that another breeder recommended us. Speaking of names, are you going to tell her yours before or after you arrive?"

Beth thought it over. If her grandmother wanted to contact her, wouldn't she have answered that letter? "Maybe I'd better wait until I'm there," she murmured. Then she pictured herself giving her name and having the door slammed in her face. "Maybe I'd better wait a few days longer . . . you know, to give her a chance to get to know me.''

Lewis's voice leaped from the receiver. "You're not thinking of going there under false pretenses!''

Beth had gone on the defensive. "No! Well . . . not really. She's hiring a dog trainer, and that's exactly who will show up. I'm not exactly going there under false *pretenses*—only under a false *name*. And if we're wrong—if she *does* know who I am and is up to something—well, she'll have to learn that two can play that game!''

That was when Lewis consulted with his wife and they pressed Beth to borrow their second car. They ended up lending her their last name as well.

The plan had seemed so simple at the time. But now, three weeks later, lying on perhaps the same bed her mother had fled years ago, Beth realized that nothing was simple about her deception. She stared at the coved ceiling. *Look how badly things have started out,* she told herself.

Ever since she had written—as Eliza Elliott—to accept the job, Beth hadn't been able to stop fantasizing about a sentimental reunion with her grandmother and her aunt. After she revealed her identity, they would explain away the rift between her mother and the two of them. Then they would ask her to call them Grandmother and Aunt Rebecca.

Beth winced. *So much for Aunt Rebecca!* Now that she thought of it, she shouldn't have expected her aunt to be called that. How confusing it would be to have two Rebeccas under the same roof. It made better sense for one of them to go by a nickname or by her middle name. According to Beth's research, her aunt was Rebecca *L.* Malvern. And now it was obvious that the "L" stood for Louisa.

Louisa Carstairs's every irritable look and phrase replayed itself in Beth's mind. *She couldn't be more opposite of Mom!*

A knock at the door roused her.

"It's Irma. Arnie and I have your luggage."

Beth let them in. Irma and her son set down Beth's suitcase and the duffel containing her training gear.

Irma went to the window. "Humph! I thought Miss High-and-Mighty closed this," she muttered. She lowered the sash so that the window remained open an inch. "There. Do you have everything you need, Eliza?"

By the time Beth realized she had not responded to her new name, Irma was making sympathetic clucking noises.

"You *are* tuckered out, aren't you?" Irma turned down the bed. "Well, these days the 'official' breakfast around here isn't till ten, so you can get a good night's sleep."

Alone again, Beth would have given anything to sprout wings and fly home to Jenny. Only, Jenny wasn't home. She was enjoying herself at a camp for developmentally disabled adults, an outing made possible by the advance check Beth had accepted for this job. She knew she couldn't afford to return the money. She'd have to stick it out.

She opened the duffel and took out a sturdy leash. It had belonged to her family's last wolfhound. Its familiar smell of leather and neat's-foot oil comforted her. *Concentrate on the dog that needs training,* she told herself, *and let the rest unfold in its own good time.*

* * *

Beth slept fitfully, caught in the vise of a recurring dream. She was running from the house, pursued in the dark by large beasts, half cougar, half human. One caught her and thrust her under the dead duff on the forest's floor. Just as she was about to suffocate, the man-beast let go of her. It had been distracted by a distant, mournful howl.

Beth bolted upright in bed. Through the cracked window came the sound of faint howling. She rose, went to the window, and opened it farther. The howling came from the north, perhaps a football field away. Was it the brindle wolfhound? Except for whimpers and groans of contentment, the huge dogs rarely made noise. Some went through life without a documented bark.

The rising, mournful sound suddenly plunged lower, then broke into a series of pained yowls. Another animal whined, then joined in the howling. In a lull between howls, Beth caught a hint of something else—a faint, tinny sound, like a single note drawn out. She strained to listen, but the sound vanished. She was certain she remembered it from earlier. When the wolfhound and mastiff tracked her from her car through the woods, that same hint of music accompanied the howling. Where did it come from?

A window opened on the floor above her. "Pipe down!" a man hollered. Beth thought it sounded like Irma's husband. He seemed tired rather than angry.

The sound ceased. Beth listened another moment, then returned to bed. She knew how to correct problem barking in dogs, but this was different. The dog doing most of the howling sounded as though he were in pain.

Beth had nearly fallen back to sleep when she thought she heard an outside door gently open, then close. The dogs had been quiet for some time. *Why would anyone go outside to check on them now? Or was someone coming in?*

This time when the dream recurred, Beth was no longer alone. Running with her from the strange beasts was a shadowy figure that remained just over her shoulder but never clearly in sight. Against her will, her legs began slowing to a shuffle. The shadowy figure slowed to keep her company even though the beasts were closing in.

"So," the figure said, speaking in a man's low voice laced with irony, "you decided to walk the rest of the way?"

The voice both comforted and perplexed her. Where had she heard it before? Beth forgot about the beasts. Was her companion taunting her? Or encouraging her to move faster?

Once Beth ignored the beasts, they dissolved into the night. So did her shadowy companion. Just before he left her in total darkness, she made out his eyes. *Bright smoke,* she murmured in her sleep, inventing her own term for such an unsettling shade of gray.

Chapter Three

Sunlight roused Beth. It streamed through the window, dissolving the cobwebs of her dreams. A burst of color caught her attention. Someone had placed on the dresser a bouquet of dahlias and chrysanthemums in every shade of yellow and orange.

Beth sat up, startled. The flowers had not been there last night. Who had brought them—and how had she managed to sleep through the intrusion? Still, she was glad for the warm colors. The room was otherwise dark or faded. Wallpaper, perhaps blue once but now a bleak gray, circled the room, disappearing by turns behind the dark and massive dresser, a tall wardrobe, a faded armchair, and the bed.

Was this Mom's room? A wave of grief threatened to overwhelm Beth. After their mother's death that winter, she had worked hard to maintain a brave front for Jenny's sake. Grieving openly had seemed too self-indulgent and would have upset Jenny's delicate hold on reality. Even now, with Jenny three hundred miles away, Beth kept up that front.

Her eyes returned to the flowers. Who had slipped in with them as she slept? Last night Irma and her son knocked and waited to be admitted. Surely they would have done so again today—as Frank Smythe would have. Louisa Carstairs didn't seem capable of anything so nice, and Rebecca Malvern, laid up with a broken hip, could not have managed the task. Louisa had mentioned having a husband and daughter, but why would they be any more welcoming than Louisa herself? Beth could think of no one else connected to the household. Then she remembered the mastiff's owner.

Her face grew warm. *Definitely not him.* Not after the way he had challenged her story about parking so far off. Until Irma had introduced her as the dog trainer, he had acted as though he suspected her of hiding something.

Beth flushed darker. *You* are *hiding something.* She grabbed her brush from the nightstand and worked her auburn hair until it snapped with electricity. She couldn't recall the last time she had slept so late. When she checked her watch, however, it was scarcely eight o'clock.

She smiled. Living in an apartment with skyscrapers blocking the horizon meant late sunrises and early sunsets. For the next few weeks the sun would take its natural course without steel and concrete in its way. She rose. Irma had said breakfast was at ten. That was far too late to get started. Beth decided to skip breakfast today and to pack along fruit and rolls tomorrow. She dressed in her working clothes—comfortable baggy jeans allowing plenty of movement, a spring-green pullover, and a khaki cotton windshell that wouldn't make those synthetic whooshes and screeches so distracting to nervous dogs. From her duffel of gear, she selected a leash, choke-chain, longe, and a tab. She stuffed them into a small backpack.

Minutes later she found her way out of a maze of wainscoted hallways and stepped into filtered morning light. Then she headed in the direction of the midnight howling. A gravel walk led through forest to a clearing. She rounded an informal hedge of tall sword ferns and drew up short.

Beyond the clearing marched a regiment of chain-link fences. Row on row led up a gentle slope to a storage room fifteen yards off. These were dog runs, with gates at each end. At most gates stood wolfhounds, mute and expectant.

Beth's heart sank. The dogs seemed to peer at her from prison cells. Although she had been hired to work with only one dog, she silently pledged to do what she could for the well-being of them all. She wondered which was her "client," and precisely what his problem was. Rebecca Malvern had been purposely vague in her correspondence, stressing that she expected Beth to judge the dog for herself. That was exactly as Beth liked it—starting with a clean slate that bore none of the owner's prejudices.

Beth rarely had this chance to meet all a given owner's dogs before the "problem dog" was singled out. She counted big, dark noses. Six wolfhounds, but she didn't find the brindle she met the night before. Nor was the mastiff anywhere to be seen. That made eight animals. She had her work cut out for her this first day. Resolutely she walked to the first run and held her hand, palm up, to the fence.

The occupant watched her hopefully. A wheaten-colored dog with darker hair outlining his face, ears, and feet, he tilted his head side to side to size up Beth. Apparently satisfied, he padded over to her and tried to wedge his massive muzzle through a small square of the fence.

Beth stroked him above his nose. "How about a walk?"

She drew the heavy bolt back, swung open the gate, and stepped inside. The dog came to her without hesitation.

"Here we go," she said, patting the dog firmly as she slipped the linked metal circle of the choke-chain over his head. Cruel as its name sounded, the choke-chain was, in Beth's experience, a kinder training device than the leather or synthetic collars most owners provided with the dogs they brought to Barking Up the Wrong Tree.

They left the run and started toward the long open area obviously laid out for training the dogs. At the far end of the grounds, Irma's son, Arnie, was doing his best to handle both the brindle wolfhound and the mastiff Beth knew from last night. She waved. Arnie hollered a greeting but kept his hands firmly on both leashes.

After a few moments in which the wolfhound tested Beth and learned his limits with her, he settled down and behaved well. "You've had expert training," Beth told him.

She didn't expect him to understand; she simply made a habit of talking to dogs as they got to know her. She wished she could let this one romp once their workout ended, but she feared he would head for Arnie and complicate his efforts with the mismatched pair he was exercising.

After a brisk warm-up with the dog heeling as she jogged and ran, Beth put him through the basic obedience drills of sit, sit-stay, down, and down-stay. She was pleased to see that he positioned himself correctly and held beautifully for the stand-for-examination as well.

"Sorry we haven't more time," she said as she returned him to his run, "but your friends could use outings too."

Beth had completed another workout and was trying to coax a shy female to make friends through the fence when a breathless Arnie Smythe joined her.

"That's Banshee. She had a bad home," he said, gasping between words. "Mrs. M threatened to take the people to court if they didn't return her. Even gave them a full refund. Banshee's still real skittish, but she's coming along."

Well, Beth told herself, *at least my grandmother feels kindly toward her animals.*

Arnie turned the mastiff and wolfhound over to Beth and entered the run. The female sidled up to him, quivering all over. Arnie petted her slowly, calming her down. Beth approved of his gentleness. She could see that with proper training Arnie would make an excellent handler.

The mastiff allowed her to lead him to his run but was no friendlier to Beth than he had been the night before. She shut him in, then turned to the brindle wolfhound.

She stroked his head. "You were enough of a gentleman last night that I'm going to trust you not to interfere with the other dogs we have out, okay?"

He gave her no problems with the next dog she worked with. This one, a smoke-colored male, fought the leash from the first minute. Beth studied his behavior. So far he seemed the most likely candidate for the problem dog she had been hired to correct.

Arnie came back with the skittish female. "It's nearly

time for breakfast,'' he told Beth. "I can put the dogs away if you want. Mrs. Carstairs is . . . well, she's particular about starting breakfast on time and about what people wear to the *big* table.'' He looked embarrassed.

Beth looked down at her cuffs and shoes, wet with dew. "Thanks for warning me. I guess I'll skip breakfasts at the 'big' table. I certainly need to start work earlier.''

Arnie smiled. "Mom figured that. She said you're welcome to eat with us.'' He dug in his pockets. "Here's a packet of jerky to hold you till I get back. Mrs. Carstairs likes to give out orders for the day the minute she finishes breakfast. We call it 'The Lineup.''' His face brightened. "Could I tell her you could use me out here today?''

Beth didn't hesitate. "Yes. Tell her I want to check out all the dogs today and could use extra help.'' She thought of the midnight howling. "I need some information, too, about what's been going on around the kennels.''

Arnie grinned. "Great! I'll be back after 'The Lineup.' Could I take Banshee along? It's good for her to be around folks more and learn to trust them.''

"You're right,'' Beth told him, smiling. "I'm glad I'll be working with someone who understands dogs so well.''

Arnie grinned and loped off with Banshee at his side.

Beth steeled herself for serious training. She had let the smoke-colored male reveal his character, but now it was time to show him who was boss. She led him to the working grounds.

"Heel,'' Beth called. And for a few steps the huge dog did just that, moving parallel to her left side, his head slightly in front. Then he forged ahead a foot, then several feet more. Prepared for this possibility, Beth had reserved five feet of slack in the leash.

Without warning, she dropped the extra length of leash and hugged the end to her chest like a halfback carrying a football. She spun to her right and started marching in the opposite direction. Beth felt the slack taken up as the unsuspecting dog continued on his headstrong way. Then, *wham!* Beth absorbed the impact as the dog ran out of leash.

She heard his yelp, one of surprise rather than pain, as she continued swiftly in her new direction. She didn't miss a step. Though the dog outweighed her, she had surprise and momentum on her side. The huge animal had no recourse but to reverse direction and hurry to catch up with her. She didn't glance at him. This training technique depended on getting the dog to observe and adjust to *her* movements, not vice versa.

This time they went farther in the correct heel position before the dog grew inattentive and lunged ahead of her. He headed for the free wolfhound watching them from his vantage point under a tree. Again Beth reversed direction; again the huge dog found himself literally at the end of his rope. Beth never broke stride. In ten minutes a well-behaved dog paced himself at her side, watching for her slightest change in course. When she stopped, he stopped and sat attentively in the correct position.

Beth walked to where she had left her backpack. From it she took the twenty-foot longe line and snapped it to the wolfhound's collar to replace the leash. Again she gave him the "heel" command and led off on a course with several more sharp turns. He moved perfectly through the course she set.

This time when she stopped, Beth patted the dog's head and released the longe line. She glanced at her watch and made a note of when twenty minutes would be up. He had earned his right to a little privacy, but dragging the longe line would serve as a valuable transition from his training session to being back on his own in his run. It took the dog a few moments to understand he was somewhat free. Finally he wandered over to the brindle wolfhound.

Two dogs to go, Beth told herself. Light-headed and hungry from skipping breakfast, she decided to take a break. She picked a spot the morning sun had cleared of dew. She sat down, drew out a strip of Arnie's jerky, and began to chew the tough yet tasty meat.

From behind her came a low, male voice. "Well, Eliza, you won that bout in the first round."

Taken by surprise, Beth swallowed a dry chunk of jerky. She knew that voice from last night. It belonged to the mastiff's owner. When she turned his way, she faced an even bigger surprise.

Blinded last night by the floodlight, she had not been able to make out his features in the brief time they spoke together. Now she gauged him to be in his late twenties. She noticed the slight cleft in his chin, the strong line of his jaw, and the dark hair framing his head with loose curls. But what riveted her attention and alarmed her were his eyes. She knew immediately just when and where she had first met them.

Beth looked quickly away from the man joining her. She couldn't believe it—he was both the "voice" from last night and the "eyes" assessing her even earlier at the accident site. Discovering he had played both those roles made her anxious, though she wasn't sure why. A night of troubled sleep had blurred her memory's edges. She knew only that she now felt doubly on guard and doubly at a disadvantage.

He smiled slightly. "I didn't mean to startle you. I only said that you won that bout with the dog."

Beth fought for composure. "It—it isn't a contest."

"True. Poor Boru didn't stand a chance."

"That's because nothing was left to *chance*. And, as you saw, the dog corrected himself." The instant Beth finished speaking, she realized how defensive she sounded.

He seemed surprised by her tone. He sat on the grass beside her. "Is that the basis of your method," he asked at last, "self-correction?"

She strove to sound more relaxed. "For many problems, yes. This dog learned that his behavior was what got him into trouble with the leash."

He looked puzzled. "Then what's the handler's role?"

"Though clearly in command, the handler plays a neutral role in the actual correction. The dog learns that the problem is his own inattention. By watching the handler and staying in the correct position, he avoids future trouble."

The newcomer frowned absently. "But isn't that deceptive? Doesn't it disguise the true situation?"

Beth squirmed at the words "deceptive" and "disguise." Was he challenging her authority or merely curious about her training methods? Was he suspicious of her, or was her secret role making her find distrust where there was none?

The dry lump of jerky was stuck halfway down her

throat and threatening her with hiccups. She tried to sound lighthearted. "Some might consider yelling at the dog or beating him to be more honest and direct. But my goal is to teach cooperation rather than frightened submission."

"Well," he said, smiling, "you're the expert."

Beth's attempt at a dignified nod was undercut by a faint hiccup. Her companion smiled wider. To Beth's consternation, she hiccupped again.

Arnie jogged into view with the female wolfhound, Banshee. "Sorry I took so long," he began. "Mrs. Carstairs was late. Mom sent you some cheese rolls and orange juice." Then he noticed Beth's companion. "Hi, Ross."

"Hi. Thanks for giving Saxon his morning run."

Arnie beamed. "No problem!"

Beth suppressed the sound of the next hiccup, but she couldn't hide the way it jolted her body.

Ross took the thermos Arnie carried. He poured out some juice. "Water would be better," he said, "but out in the field we take what we can find for such emergencies."

Beth motioned for the juice, but Ross pulled it out of reach. "Not yet," he said, in feigned severity. "First take ten deep, swift breaths. Hyperventilation is the key."

Beth suppressed another hiccup. "I thought medics stuck to blood pressure and tourniquets," she said.

Ross looked momentarily perplexed; then he threw Arnie a grin. "The top three in the class get this training," he said. "Hey, I granted you expertise in dog-handling— you could at least allow me a little know-how in hiccup relief."

Beth smiled and took the required deep breaths. When she finished, she felt giddy.

"Hold your breath," Ross told her, "until I finish counting." He caught up her wrist and felt for the pulse.

Beth held her breath as directed and tried to count the number of times her pulse leaped to his fingers.

"Now," he said, at last, "drink slowly. Try not to breathe until you've emptied the cup."

She complied. When she finished, her hiccups were gone. When she handed back the cup, however, she faked a little hiccup. Then she laughed, giving her ruse away.

"You had me worried for a second," Ross said. "That's supposed to be a surefire remedy."

"You *really* learn that in your training?" she asked.

Smiling wider, Ross shook his head. "No, this remedy's a matter of family honor—I learned it from my grandmother."

The three of them sat a moment in silence, watching the two male wolfhounds, the dark one still trailing the longe. They sniffed a slow trail around the edge of the training field. The female wolfhound slipped up to Beth and gave her the once-over that Beth accepted as a prelude to friendship.

For the first time since her arrival, Beth felt content rather than uneasy. She was doing the work she had been hired to do. For the moment everything was aboveboard.

Arnie asked about the longe line the smoke-colored dog trailed behind him. Beth explained its function and checked her watch. She told Arnie the line could come off, and he went to release the dog.

"He'd make a good dog handler," she said absently.

Ross looked sharply at her. "How good?"

Beth was surprised at the intensity of his question. "From what I've seen this morning, very good."

"You can tell that already?"

"Well, he has a natural disposition for the work—"

"But it takes more than that?"

She nodded. "Determination and a willingness to do the hard, repetitive work as well as its more rewarding phases."

"How soon could you be certain Arnie has the aptitude?"

"Well, if he could give me a hand every day—"

Ross nodded. "I'm sure it can be arranged."

"I can tell this is important to you. Why?"

He drew a long breath. "It's more important to Arnie and to his parents. He has a learning disability and barely graduated from high school this year."

"Oh! I assumed he was much younger!"

Ross nodded. "That's another problem. People treat him as young as he looks, sending the message that he isn't yet ready to accomplish much. As for that learning disability, if it had been diagnosed earlier, he could have gone to a school with special programs."

Beth thought of Jenny. "Yes," she murmured, "special programs. I suppose his parents couldn't afford them?"

Ross shook his head. "No, that, too, could have been arranged. But Arnie loves it here. I'm not certain his parents could have talked him into leaving the place."

"Does he have to leave?" Beth asked, thinking of her sister and the half-day program for autistic adults beginning next month in Berkeley. Transporting Jenny there and back would be a minor problem compared to getting Jenny adjusted to the change in her safe, familiar routine.

Ross nodded. "He needs to lose his fear of leaving, even if he decides to return. And he needs an occupation, preferably one with oral rather than written training. He needs something he loves to do and is good at." A weary look settled onto his face. "We all need that."

Beth sensed something behind his words but suppressed her impulse to question him. It wasn't fair to pry into his thoughts when she planned to keep secret so many of her own.

His eyes searched hers. "Could you work with Arnie enough to assess his chances at succeeding at dog training?"

"Yes. I've trained several others for the work."

"Nothing official. Arnie mustn't know he's on trial."

Her eyes widened. "But it wouldn't be right to keep it from him!"

Arnie came into earshot, ending the conversation. Both wolfhounds trotted at his side. The brindle dog headed straight for Beth. He gave her cheek a swipe of his tongue before settling next to her and rolling onto his back.

She laughed. He looked like an overturned coffee table with crooked legs. Clearly he wanted her to scratch his massive chest. When she finished, the dog grunted contentedly and flopped onto his side. He stretched until over seven feet separated his front paws from his back ones.

Beth asked Arnie about the howling the night before.

He shrugged. "Pop and I can't figure it out. Lurgan— this one—started that a month ago. Pop thinks maybe a strange animal smell coming from the woods bothers him."

"Can you remember Lurgan doing it before?" Beth asked.

Arnie shook his head. "Nope."

"You could have fooled me," Ross interjected. "That dog has serenaded us almost nightly since I've been here."

"Yeah," Arnie said, "but he never did it before that."

Beth made a mental note that Ross was a visitor too, then returned to the task at hand. "Mrs. Malvern wrote that she broke her hip in June. How did it happen?"

Arnie looked worried. "She fell down the stairs."

"Mrs. Carstairs told me that two people saw the dog *attack* her mother."

Arnie frowned. "Mrs. M says it isn't true."

"What do you think?" Beth persisted.

"I don't think Lurgan did it—at least not on purpose."

A whistle shrilled from the house.

"Three blasts," Arnie said. "That means I have to report for chores. Oh, Mrs. Carstairs said I can't help you. She says there's too much gardening for me to do."

"Well," Beth said, "I really need an extra pair of hands. I'll take it up with Mrs. Malvern."

Arnie brightened. "Really? You think she'll let me?"

Beth glanced at Ross as she borrowed his phrase from moments before. "I'm sure it can be arranged." She rose to her feet. "You report to Mrs. Carstairs for now, Arnie. I've got two dogs left before I call it a morning."

"Oh, I keep forgetting to give you these," Arnie said. He dug into his pockets and pulled out Beth's car keys.

Beth accepted them. "I take it I won't have to park so far away next time."

Arnie looked perplexed.

"The barrier—a sawhorse—I told you about," she said.

He glanced worriedly at Ross. "We never saw one."

Beth's eyes widened. "But there *was* a barrier—that's the only reason I parked where I did!"

Arnie looked down. "There wasn't one."

The whistle shrilled at closer range and sent Arnie on his way. Louisa Carstairs stood at the clearing's edge. Beth was surprised to see her there so quickly from the house. Louisa had covered a lot of ground in a short time to let Arnie know that her whistle meant business.

Ross stood. "Maybe you made a simple mistake." With that he turned and walked toward the house.

An hour later Beth was finishing up with the last dog who needed a workout. Though rusty on the finer points of leash-handling, this male was otherwise as well trained as the female Beth had just put through her paces. She was glad this wolfhound was easy to handle, for she knew she wasn't concentrating well enough to deal with a problem dog. She couldn't get the disappearing sawhorse out of her mind. It seemed a little thing, but clearly it undermined Ross's and Arnie's confidence in her wits, if not her integrity.

Last night she had been road weary and jumpy enough to see a boogeyman in the woods, yet she was positive she hadn't imagined the sawhorse blocking the road. It *was* there. But what happened to it? Who would remove it—and why?

As she walked the dog back to his run, she noticed a middle-aged stranger observing her. Once the dog was in his pen, the short, silver-haired man approached Beth. Light of build and dressed in a crisp linen suit, he appeared to be in his early sixties. His well-preserved and otherwise handsome looks were marred by salt-and-pepper eyebrows that strained in a rigid arch high over his eyes. To Beth he looked as out of place among the redwoods as a logger would look in San Francisco's financial district.

He introduced himself as Paul Carstairs, Louisa's husband. "I'm out for a walk," he said. "It's good for my sciatica." He gingerly touched his right hip. "Sometimes I'll be sitting in a restaurant and the pain becomes so *killing,* I simply must get out to walk, walk, walk it off."

Beth realized he had been standing still as they talked. "Please don't let me keep you from doing so."

He offered her a polite but stiff smile. "Oh, I'm here on a mission as well. Your presence was missed at breakfast. I've come to escort you to lunch."

"Thank you," Beth said, "but I'll be taking meals with the Smythes. That way I won't waste dog-training time on changing my clothes to eat with the family."

"Come as you are to this one," he replied, bending swiftly to flick a twig from the top of his polished shoe.

"It's generous of your wife to make an exception for me," Beth said wryly.

"Oh, it's not Louisa's idea. This is a command performance ordered by your employer, my mother-in-law."

Beth drew a deep breath. *This is it,* she told herself. *Prepare to meet your grandmother.*

When Beth reached the house with Paul Carstairs, Irma informed them that lunch would be delayed an hour so a trio of newcomers could join them.

Paul stiffened when he learned his daughter was in the party. "Georgia? But she wasn't due back for a month!"

Beth remembered hearing Paul and Louisa's daughter mentioned last night, but now that fact took on new meaning. *I'm about to meet a cousin!* She felt excited and happy.

"Well, ex-*cuse* me!" Irma muttered as Paul walked briskly away. "Some folks might be a little happier to learn their only child was on her way home."

Beth now had time to shower and change before meeting her grandmother. She wanted to look businesslike yet casual, in keeping with her casual business. The depth of her anxiety to make a good first impression surprised her.

A half hour later she smoothed her lapis-blue tunic over matching raw-silk slacks. She was growing more nervous by the minute. The room seemed to shrink inward on her, shifting the whole weight of the house onto her shoulders.

She stepped into the corridor and headed toward the distant sounds of voices and clinking glasses. She passed two doorways and was about to pass another when she heard a sound halfway between a bird's chirp and a hiss.

Er-psst! psst!

Beth looked to her right. A door was partly open. An elderly woman seated inside that room beckoned to Beth.

"In here!" the woman called. Then she laughed, a cheerful, tinkling sound like bells with muffled clappers.

Beth entered and closed the door as directed.

The woman sat in an armchair near the window. She wore a bright housecoat and had a daffodil-colored comforter spread over her lap and legs. When the door was shut, she made a gesture of dismissal in the direction of the front of the house. Except for pronounced laugh lines around her mouth and eyes, her skin looked as soft and unblemished as rose petals. Only her hair and bent fingers betrayed her age. She smiled. "Did you like the flowers?"

Beth smiled back. "They were from you?"

The woman nodded. "I had hoped for a little chat then. But you looked so tired and solemn, I let you sleep. Well, now I have you for a bit before all the folderol starts."

Folderol! Beth's eyes stung. *Mom used to say that when she was having fun and pretending to be old-fashioned!* Beth searched the older woman's face. *Are you . . . are you truly my grandmother?* she wondered.

All cheer leeched from her companion's expression. She looked suddenly frail. "Oh, dear! Are you all right?"

"Yes," Beth said. "Just something in my eye."

The woman handed Beth a cotton handkerchief and smiled. Once again she looked young and carefree. "Well, then, let me begin by telling you how nice it is to see a fresh face around here—especially such a young and pretty one. Now, tell me what you've been up to."

Beth had barely begun to describe her sessions with the dogs when her hostess interrupted her.

"But that's *business,* my dear!" She wrinkled her nose. "You'll have plenty of time later to go over all *that.* I want to hear about *you.* I take it you're not married?"

The question surprised and puzzled Beth. "No."

"Engaged? Seeing someone special these days?"

Beth chose her words carefully. "No. I'm responsible for my . . . for a family member with special needs. I don't have much free time."

"Well, bless your heart!" the woman cried. "But I

hope you aren't creating more tasks for yourself than necessary. Believe me, I know what it's like to have a grandchild hovering over your every need." She shook a bent finger at Beth. "It's all I can manage to talk a certain young person into taking an evening off now and then. And the next thing you know, the stubborn dear is back early to check on me!"

Beth remembered Paul Carstairs's irritation at learning his daughter was "back early."

"Anyway," the woman continued, "maybe the two of you could get out of here and have some fun together."

Beth didn't know what to say. Had she been hired to entertain and draw out a retiring girl as well as to train a difficult dog? Taking money to be kind to her own cousin was unthinkable.

A tinny bell clinked impatiently in the distance.

Beth's hostess sighed. "Louisa and her whistles, bells, and gongs! The grand banquet is about to begin. Could you give me a boost up, my dear? I have trouble navigating out of these low chairs."

Beth searched the room for equipment. "Are you still using a wheelchair? Or have you graduated to a walker?"

The woman laughed. "I may be stiff with arthritis, but a walker would be a *demotion* rather than a *graduation!*" With that she threw herself forward to rise on her own.

"But your hip!" Beth cried, quickly coming to her aid.

At first the woman looked bewildered; then she laughed. "Oh, dear! Do you mean to say you took me for the *dog* lady?"

Beth blinked at her.

"Oh, but this is wonderful! Until this very moment

we made it clear through life without ever once being mistaken for each other! Oh, dear, I really should have introduced myself immediately."

Beth's heart sank. "You're not Rebecca Malvern?"

"No, my dear. I just assumed you had already met Rebecca. I'm Jenny Trenton, her sister."

Tension ruled the air in the dining room. No one spoke after Rebecca Malvern sent word to start the luncheon without her. Her place at the head of the table remained empty, as did two additional places. In the distance, muffled by a closed door, two women's voices shrilled at each other.

Beth listlessly worked at her salad. For the fraction of time she believed Jenny Trenton to be her grandmother, she had felt ecstatic, like a lost child who hears a familiar voice. That illusion shattered, she now ached with disappointment. *At least she's my great-aunt,* Beth tried to console herself. *And Jenny is her namesake.*

Everyone else present was at least twice Beth's age. She wondered where Ross was and realized she neither knew his last name nor how he was connected to this odd household so full of surprises. She was grateful she sat next to Jenny. Despite Jenny's restricted and obviously painful movement, she radiated joy.

The only new face at the table belonged to Yvonne Sanderson, a stark woman in her late sixties. She wore her dyed black hair drawn back into a no-nonsense French roll. She kept looking nervously in the direction of the distant argument.

Jenny broke the silence. In a whisper the whole table could hear, she explained to Beth that Yvonne was Rebecca's stepdaughter, George Malvern's only child from his first marriage. Jenny pointed to the place reserved for Yvonne's son and added, ''Matt's about your age.''

Yvonne snapped to attention. ''Why, Aunt Jen! You know Matt's nearly thirty. This girl is barely twenty.''

''Twenty-three,'' Beth murmured.

Jenny looked mischievous. ''Oh, dear, so he is! I always think of him as much younger. People who go on and on at getting their education always seem that way.''

Yvonne dabbed at the corner of her mouth with her linen napkin. ''Why should Matt settle for the first thing that comes along? He needs a major he can relate to.''

''Well,'' Jenny said, ''better late than never.''

Beth stole a glance at Yvonne. *George Malvern's daughter by a previous marriage? That makes her Mom's half-sister . . . and my aunt!*

When she had researched her family, Beth worked backward through time to George and Rebecca Malvern's marriage and had given no thought to her grandparents' lives before that date. Yet here was proof that her grandfather had had another life before he married Rebecca. *How little I know about Mom's background—about my own flesh and blood.*

Footsteps approached the dining room. Yvonne looked far over Beth's head and beamed. ''There you are!''

In strode a lanky man who indeed looked younger than thirty. He swept a choirboy's shock of sandy hair from his forehead and headed for the chair next to Yvonne's.

''Rough going?'' his mother asked him.

''Georgie's catching the worst of it. She was driving.'' Again he pushed back his mop of hair. About to take his seat, he noticed Beth and sent her a smile that suggested this choirboy smuggled frogs into church under his robe.

Paul Carstairs roused from his soup to make a stiff ritual of introducing Beth. As if to mock his uncle's formality, Matt reached over the table. Beth expected a handshake, but Matt bent over her hand and kissed it.

Louisa gasped and dropped her spoon. Paul cleared his throat repeatedly. As Matt sat down, his mother gave Beth a severe look of dismissal.

Down the hall, a door slammed. Seconds later a young woman stormed into the room. She sported expertly high-lighted hair and a sundress so white, it emphasized how flushed her face now was. She threw Matt a nasty glance.

Again Paul made the introductions, presenting Beth to his daughter, Georgia Carstairs. Georgia gave Beth a perfunctory nod, sat down, and began stabbing her salad.

Beth smiled to herself. This was not the shy, retiring cousin she had imagined. But that had been when she assumed Georgia was the considerate and self-sacrificing grandchild Jenny Trenton wanted entertained.

Because Beth's father was eighteen years older than her mother, Beth's cousins on his side of the family had been too old to play with. Here at last was the cousin her own age that she had always longed for. She immediately decided to give Georgia the benefit of the doubt. *Maybe she's fun to be with when she isn't so angry.*

Beth glanced at Matt. *He seems nice and is a cousin, too—or a half-cousin? This is so confusing!*

Matt caught her looking at him and smiled. "If Georgie and I can wheedle Rebecca into letting you off early one day, how about our all going out together?" He ignored the murderous glance Georgia threw him. "That way I won't have to play third wheel on Georgia's bicycle."

Georgia's frown slowly cleared. "Matt, you *do* have

your inspired moments.'' She turned a crisp smile on
Beth. ''Yes, please come, Eliza. It'll be fun.''

Beth didn't understand Matt and Georgia's cozy short-
hand, but she agreed to the outing if she could get far
enough ahead in her work to earn the time off.

As the meal progressed, Beth's hopes picked up. So
far she had met five blood relatives. One, Jenny Trenton,
or ''Aunt Jen,'' as everyone at the table called her, was
wonderful. Maybe some others would turn out to be nice
too. Silently she practiced their titles. *Great-Aunt Jen,
Aunt Louisa, Aunt Yvonne, Cousin Matt, Cousin Georgia.*

Not until Beth was summoned to the den did she remember who had been missing from her litany— *Grandmother.*

The room to which Irma showed Beth was on the
deeply shaded side of the house. Dark wainscoting made
the study even gloomier. The gleaming steel of Rebecca
Malvern's wheelchair seemed out of place amid the dark
oak furniture.

She appeared as uncompromising and unhappy as her
sister was accommodating and cheerful. A gaunt woman
nearing eighty, she wore her thick, white hair in a low
bun. She looked too strong to be trapped, even temporarily, in the wheelchair in which she now sat. Large and
steady, her hands straightened and restraightened a leather
dog leash.

''You've rested sufficiently from your journey,'' she
said, not bothering to look at Beth. ''It's time to get down
to business on the work for which you're being well
paid.''

Beth stiffened. ''The four hours I put in this morning
with the dogs were a good start.''

Rebecca's colorless eyes met Beth's for a long moment. "Dog*s?*" She hissed the final *s*. "You were hired to work with a single dog, not to play with them all."

Beth kept an even tone despite the butterflies in her stomach. "Putting all the kennels' dogs through their paces can save time with the problem dog by revealing a training flaw." Knowing that most owners considered such an approach a luxury they could not afford, she now braced herself for just such a response.

But Rebecca dismissed the topic with a snort of disgust. "And just what have you discovered about my dogs?"

"Presently they are underexercised and losing the finer points of their obviously excellent training."

Rebecca scowled. "I haven't been able to oversee their handling since my accident. Oh, Irma's boy makes sure they get exercised, but that's not the same."

"It could be. With instruction, Arnie would make a fine handler. I could use his help. If you can spare him from his other duties, I could teach him the basics."

Rebecca nodded. "Use the boy, then." She stretched a length of the leash taut between her two fists. "And what about your chief assignment?"

Beth shook her head. "No one has pointed out your problem dog—nor have I wanted that done before I had the chance to handle or observe all the wolfhounds. I haven't yet worked with Banshee or Lurgan, but they seemed well behaved when Arnie exercised them. The one named Boru tested me the most. Is he the one?"

Rebecca laughed triumphantly and reached to the desk beside her for the phone. She pressed a single button. "Frank? Are any hounds hiding out from Louisa in the kitchen? Good. Bring along—'' She broke off and glanced at Beth. "You know which one to bring." Then she turned from the phone and sat straighter in her wheelchair. "If a trainer can't pick out the right dog, it proves he's not the savage beast Louisa claims he is."

Footsteps, both human and canine, approached the door.

"Come in!" Rebecca boomed. She shook a finger at Beth. "Take a good look at the one my daughter tried to have destroyed while I was under the knife for this hip."

Beth turned as the door opened. There stood Frank Smythe with the first Malvern wolfhound Beth had met. She gasped. "Not Lurgan!"

Rebecca called the dog. The wolfhound padded straight to his mistress and licked her outstretched hand with his enormous tongue. "Down," she said, and the dog obeyed, lowering himself slowly next to the wheelchair.

Rebecca threw Beth a haughty, defiant look. "Well? What do you think of your 'dangerous' client now?"

Beth shook her head in disbelief. "As I told you, I haven't handled him officially. But he's the one I've spent the most time around and the one I would least expect—"

"My point exactly!" the older woman cried.

Beth lowered her voice. "But I was about to say that he does have problems. For one thing, there's his howling."

Rebecca doubled the leash back on itself so that two lengths stretched between her fists. Then she brought her fists together until the two strips of leash separated to form a wide "O." Suddenly she jerked her hands apart. Leather slapped leather with a loud *crack!*

Beth jumped. The wolfhound's head swiveled toward the sound. Though it had been as sudden as gunshot and nearly as loud, Lurgan watched his mistress with absolute trust.

"Howling indeed!" Rebecca cried. "What *makes* him howl is the problem. Your job is to uncover it."

"And your accident?" Beth asked. "Did he cause it?"

Rebecca dropped the leash. "Lies!" She clutched the armrests of her wheelchair until her knuckles shone white. "Lies meant to get me to sell my kennels!"

Beth turned to see Frank Smythe's reaction to this accusation. The doorway was empty. Apparently he had slipped away before his employer's anger could explode.

Rebecca was clearly worked up. Her head shook slightly. Two wisps of white hair had slipped from her bun and now stood out from her head like forked lightning. Her eyes narrowed, nearly vanishing in her contorted features.

"I was about to enter my first dog show in years," she muttered. "Lurgan was to establish Malvern Kennels as a leader in the breeding world once more. And then *this!*" She indicated her hip. "No use crying over spilt milk. I have a dog you must bring up to snuff before the big shows. Work with the others when you can, and remember this: You are not being paid to listen to lies." She leaned forward and glared at Beth. "Nor are you here to conspire with those who would sell the kennels out from under me!"

Beth stared in amazement. Where had this sudden hostility and suspicion come from? And why was she its present target? *Does this woman know my secret, after all?*

Rebecca flicked on her chair's motor. She wheeled halfway around, turning her back on Beth and leaving no doubt that the interview was over.

Beth walked to her room. With each step her knees felt more and more like rubber. Rebecca Malvern's anger echoed in her ears. Beth thought of her sister locked in her private world. Was there any reason to hope for help and understanding from this grandmother?

Poor Jenny! Beth thought. She barely made it to her room before the tears began to fall.

Chapter Four

Dinner that evening did nothing to lessen Beth's disappointment in having at last met her grandmother. The meal was a sullen affair, with Louisa and Yvonne pointedly not speaking and Georgia pouting for an undisclosed reason. Even the cheerful Jenny appeared subdued. Beth caught something about Aunt Jen's grandchild canceling out of dinner, but she hadn't wanted to pry further.

Matt Sanderson provided some relief by rolling his eyes at the awkward formality at the table and by attempting to engage Beth in conversation. His mother, Yvonne, invariably interrupted those efforts, behaving as though she didn't want her son fraternizing with the hired help.

Beth caught herself wishing the other visitor, Ross, were there. *At least he's interesting to talk to.*

Rebecca Malvern sat sternly at her table's head, ignoring her son-in-law's attempts to be gracious to her and to her alone. Clearly used to her rebuffs, Paul Carstairs took no notice of them and continued to play the gallant.

If this is what it means to have a big family, Beth tried to comfort herself, *who needs it?*

She did learn one new fact about her grandmother: No one dared to call her that. When they found it necessary to address her directly, both Georgia and Matt called her Rebecca. Just as dessert began, Georgia slipped up and referred to a household car as "Grandmother's Buick."

Louisa gasped. Forks froze in midair. Rebecca set down her cup with a loud *clink!* and stared over Georgia's head for a long, tense moment before wheeling back from the table and exiting the room. The whir of her wheelchair's motor disappeared down the hall before anyone dared speak.

Paul broke the silence with a single word. "Georgia!"

At first his daughter looked miserable. Then she jutted out her chin, threw her linen napkin onto the table, and bolted from the room. Paul turned a reproachful stare on his wife. Louisa cringed and turned pale.

Beth was seeing her aunt in a new light. She wondered if Louisa was so high-handed with the Smythes as a reaction to her own family situation. There, Louisa was caught between a rock and a hard place—her mother and husband.

"I'm stiffer than usual today," Aunt Jen said, winking at Beth. "Would you mind giving me an arm back to my room?"

Beth was happy to leave the tension of the dining room. When Aunt Jen asked Irma to send a pot of tea and two cups to her room, Beth realized she was in for a cozy visit.

"What you must think of us!" Aunt Jen exclaimed once they reached her room. "We can be pleasant enough when we've a mind to. Are you warm? I'm always chilly here."

She settled painfully into her armchair. Beth found the cheerful comforter and tucked it around Aunt Jen's legs.

"Thank you, dear. I wish it were that easy to correct the chill at the dinner table! You happen to be here at a particularly awkward time. And poor Yvonne's visit doesn't help matters—not that I'm blaming her, mind you. There's always been bad blood between Yvonne and Louisa. Their children have managed to get along, but those sisters haven't exchanged a word in twenty years. In fact, I can't remember the last time they've been together under the same roof. Something must be brewing! Usually Louisa clears out when Yvonne is scheduled to pay one of her duty calls here."

"Sibling rivalry?" Beth asked.

"Not in the usual sense. Their father is partly to blame. He wasn't sure that Rebecca would do the right thing for the daughter by his previous marriage. So he set up a trust fund for Yvonne but left such vague instructions that Rebecca still manages the money and doles it out as she pleases. George left Yvonne this house and its furnishings, though he willed Rebecca the use of it for life."

"And the kennels?" Beth asked.

"They're on Rebecca's property—that's why they're such a hearty walk from the house. My sister couldn't bear the thought of Yvonne tearing down the kennels when she finally gets this place. The moment Rebecca dies, Yvonne takes possession of the house. Because it's been hers, technically, since her father's death, Yvonne's spent her life thinking of Rebecca and her tribe as squatters."

Beth wanted to learn something about her mother's childhood. "He left nothing to his other children?"

Aunt Jen shook her head. "Since their mother, Rebecca, was living, everything else went to her. Yvonne has only the acre this house sits on. That leaves over two hundred more acres to the estate. At the time of George's death, they were worth about what the house was, but nowadays the timber alone must be worth millions.''

Beth tried again. ''So Yvonne and . . . and your sister's children are at odds over their inheritance?''

Aunt Jen sighed. ''It runs deeper than that, and there's only Yvonne and Louisa left. Rebecca received word that her younger daughter died earlier this year.'' She looked sad. ''But to answer your question: When George married Rebecca, Yvonne was packed off to boarding school. Thus she and Louisa were raised apart, and they didn't have the chance to battle problems out the way Rebecca and I did as youngsters. That's why things go relatively smoothly between my sister and me in our golden years. All the scratches and bruises are long healed and forgotten.''

''You get along with *her?*'' Beth had blurted it out before she realized how rude it sounded.

But Aunt Jen only laughed. ''My, yes. Especially when we're alone. Oh, I don't tangle with Rebecca when she's on the warpath, but I know my own mind. I can manage her quite to my own satisfaction—when it's for her own good. We all need to feel comfortable with *someone,* and Rebecca's only human. She's always turned to me when the going got rough.''

''So you're here only temporarily? And out of pity?''

Aunt Jen shook her head. ''Rebecca has offered me a permanent home, but I haven't decided whether to accept. As for pity—well, that's only a tiny part of why I moved in after Rebecca's fall. This is difficult to explain to someone your age—heaven knows I've tried and failed to do so with my own grandchildren! You have to realize that my sister and I share a wealth of memories. She's the only person alive with whom I can discuss our parents—without hearing them treated as historical artifacts.''

''I see,'' Beth said softly.

Aunt Jen's eyes misted. ''Rebecca remembers how Mama made bread, how Papa told us his stories by the woodstove. Talking over those times with someone who's shared them keeps the precious moments *alive* instead of letting them fade to dusty anecdotes to tell our children.''

''I'm sure your children love hearing them,'' Beth said quietly. ''I wish I knew more about my great-grandparents.''

''Watch out!'' Aunt Jen warned. ''That borders on an open invitation for me to tell you my stories. But I didn't drag you here to use you as a listening post. I want to make up for that interrupted dessert. When the tea comes, we can share some cookies my granddaughter baked.'' She pointed to a tin on the dresser.

Beth rose to fetch it. Reaching for the tin, she noticed a framed photograph nearby. It was a standard studio photo of a family of four. From the look of the wife's hairstyle and dress, the picture was nearly twenty years old. It was the husband who drew Beth's attention. His dark hair and good looks seemed vaguely familiar.

''That's *my* tribe,'' Aunt Jen said. ''Bring them along to the party. After all, we'll be eating Alice's cookies. She's the little sweetheart in the photo. All grown now.''

''Yes,'' Beth added, ''the one you expected at dinner.''

''Heavens, no! Alice is married and raising her brood

on the other side of the continent. I don't see her nearly as often as I'd like. This Christmas perhaps.''

Someone knocked at the door. Beth juggled the photo and the tin of cookies as she opened the door for Irma.

When she and Aunt Jen were sipping tea and munching homemade gingersnaps, Beth remembered the photo. She set it up so that it faced Aunt Jen. To be polite, Beth asked which of the adults in the photograph was Aunt Jen's child.

Aunt Jen's bell-like laugh lingered in the air. ''Both! I always tell Shirley she's as much my daughter as Al Junior is my son. He was adopted, you see, so Shirley is as much a blood relative as my own boy—as if blood matters one iota when it comes to family! It certainly hasn't made Rebecca's any happier. Anyway, Al Junior was all Al Senior and I had until our son had the good sense and taste to find Shirley and marry her. We couldn't have chosen better ourselves!''

''She must love her mother-in-law's attitude.''

Aunt Jen took no notice of the compliment. She put down her cup and pointed to the picture. ''Alice you've met, through her cookies, so that leaves her brother.'' She cast Beth a mischievous look. ''*He's* the one I was hoping to introduce you to at dinner. You remember— the one I mentioned this morning? The grandchild who works, works, works and then squanders his free time on fussing over me?''

''Oh!'' Beth said. ''I pictured a grand*daughter*.''

''Anyway,'' Aunt Jen continued, ''he's on call and had to respond to an emergency. But tomorrow you're sure to finally meet Ross.''

Beth dropped her cookie. Her eyes widened.

"Oh, dear," Aunt Jen said. "Something tells me you've already met my Ross. And from your looks, it wasn't all moonlight and roses."

Beth recovered her cookie and composure as well. "More like moonlight and mastiffs," she said with forced levity. "I couldn't see him properly last night and didn't realize then I'd seen him even earlier."

Aunt Jen frowned slightly. "I'm confused. You met Ross even before you arrived here?"

"Well, we didn't quite *meet*. We simply saw each other on my way here—at the site of a car accident." Beth grew silent, thinking, *That's when he first looked at me so suspiciously.*

"Oh!" Aunt Jen said. "That must have been the emergency call he answered yesterday. A minor accident. Just scratches and bruises, he said."

Beth nodded. "Still, that woman was lucky to be attended so quickly by a medic."

"A medic? Not in this neck of the woods. In the month he's been here, Ross has always worked alone."

"But—" Beth faltered. "But isn't that what your grandson does for a living?"

"Dear, no! Not unless he's fibbed about those years of study and sacrifice when he hardly had a moment to visit me." She shook a finger at the boy in the photo. "Why, Ross Trenton, I'll disown you if you didn't use that time to become a doctor like we all thought!"

Beth flushed to remember the wry look on Ross's face when she had offhandedly referred to his medic's training. *He let me believe he was something he isn't! Why, he's as bad as—* Her face grew even hotter. *As bad as me!*

"Whatever is the matter?" Aunt Jen exclaimed.

Beth didn't know what to say.

Aunt Jen studied her. "It's that rascal Ross, isn't it?" she said at last. "Dear me, and I was *so* hoping the two of you would hit it off!"

Beth walked the grounds before turning in for the night. She had a lot to think about. Her family was nothing like she had imagined. For one thing, it was larger and far more complicated. For another, she saw little hope of being welcomed into its arms, certainly not into those of either aunt. As jealously as Louisa and Yvonne regarded each other, how would they feel about new relatives? She suspected they would view Jenny and her as additional rivals for Rebecca's favor and money.

The sun disappeared into a red haze to the west. Beth headed back, following a path leading to a side of the house she hadn't explored. *Rebecca Malvern won't welcome Jenny and me, either. She has all the grandmotherly instincts of a snake. Look how she ignores Matt and Georgia. There's no point in letting her know who I am. She won't care about Jenny. If only she were more like Aunt Jen!*

At the thought of Aunt Jen, Beth's hopes stirred. *If Aunt Jen decides to move on after Rebecca's recovery, I could write her and tell her everything. She would understand why I hid my identity. Just having her as a pen pal would mean I could salvage something worthwhile from this . . . this wild grandmother chase.*

"A penny for your thoughts."

Beth was so lost in her reflections, she hadn't seen the figure ahead of her. Matt Sanderson stood in her path.

Even the dim twilight could not hide the gleam of his smile.

"You startled me," she said.

Matt chuckled. "Better me than the pond." He pointed ahead. "It's just a small artificial pond next to the house, but you looked like you were marching straight for it. I fell in myself as a kid. Bobbing for goldfish."

Now Beth noticed the slick of dark water ahead. "Small! I've seen smaller swimming pools!"

He laughed. "Well, it's wide but only two or three feet deep. Here, I'll show you. Only, we have to whisper. This is forbidden territory these days."

She lowered her voice. "Forbidden?"

"Yes. It's Rebecca's hideout for her midday nap—only, we all pretend she isn't taking one. Napping's something old people do, and Rebecca refuses to grow old. That's why we're forbidden to come here, especially after lunch. We mustn't see the *grande dame* catching forty winks!"

They walked to the pond's edge. Beth saw what Matt meant about marching into the water. She might have done just that if he hadn't been there to warn her.

The pond was nearly flush with the ground. Ferns lined its edge in some places, large rocks in others, making the pond appear a natural body of water. The only thing that didn't fit the scene was a huge deck stretching from the house to jut over one end of the pond. The lumber was new enough to glow softly in the fading light. Double doors led from the house onto the deck.

Matt pointed to a stack of lumber at the edge of the deck. "Rebecca had Frank dismantle the railing as soon as the building inspector approved the addition," he whispered. "She said it marred her view from the wheelchair."

"But that's dangerous," Beth whispered back.

"And against the Building Code, but don't try to tell *her* that. Not unless you're wearing a hard hat."

"It sounds like she hasn't been an ideal grandmother."

Matt shrugged. "My brother and I never counted as grandchildren."

"I'm sorry."

"Don't be. We had it better than poor Georgie. Rebecca just ignored my brother and me. Everything Georgie did was wrong. We wouldn't have traded places with her as official grandkids for anything."

Beth studied his face in the dying light. "You like your cousin, don't you? You seem close."

Matt shrugged again. "Sure, I like Georgie. My brother and I spent summer vacations here with her. He and I are ten years apart, but Georgie's only two years younger than me. So when my brother went his way, she and I hung out together. Georgie and I learned to run interference for each other." He chuckled softly. "We still do. I guess you could say we're close. She's like a sister who's always off at boarding school. It's fun to get together."

Beth felt sad as they strolled around to the front door. "I never knew my cousins."

Matt looked at Beth as if waiting for her to explain. When she didn't, he shrugged good-naturedly. Beth said good night and abruptly left.

Chapter Five

The next day Beth threw herself into her work. To escape her own problems, she immersed herself in those of the wolfhounds. One problem was the midnight howling. It had awakened her again. She vowed to get to the bottom of it, even if it meant keeping watch all night at the kennels.

Beth worked with two dogs before she turned to Lurgan. "I can't understand it," she told Arnie, who took over each wolfhound after she put it through a rigorous initial routine. "Lurgan's given us the least trouble of all. Mrs. Malvern's fall must have been a freak accident."

Lurgan, in fact, was so well behaved on the training field that Beth decided he was too used to working there. She planned to test him later by taking him to a setting where he wasn't used to being on a leash. She asked Arnie to work without her after lunch, exercising the remaining wolfhounds just as he had seen her do that morning. He eagerly agreed.

They returned to the house for lunch. Beth was enjoying sharing hers with all three Smythes when a loud crash in the distance drew them all to the living room.

There, dirt and shards of china littered the wood floor. A fern sprawled on a nearby rug, its mass of roots exposed. In the far corner of the room cowered Lurgan.

Beth called Lurgan to her side. Clearly disturbed by the mishap, he shook until she calmed him by stroking his head and back.

"Poor fellow," Irma said. She picked up the fern. "A new pot and it'll be good as new."

"Good as new!" Louisa Carstairs stood framed in the double doorway leading to the dining room. "That fern stand was over a century old! It belonged to my grandmother!"

Irma handed the fern to Arnie, who appeared glad to have an excuse to leave. He softly called Lurgan. The dog followed him. No one else spoke.

The motor of Rebecca's wheelchair broke the tense silence. She coasted into view beyond her daughter. "What is it now?" she asked crossly.

"I'll tell you what it is now!" Louisa whined. "It's one swipe of Lurgan's tail—and a family heirloom is gone!"

"We'll clear it right up," Irma's husband said. He threw Louisa a hard stare that made her start.

Rebecca waved her hand in a gesture of dismissal. "Finish your hot meal, Frank. The dirt won't go anywhere in the next hour. And stop your hysterics, Louisa. You always hated that fern stand. Nothing but stark modern furniture for you."

Louisa's nostrils flared. "But it's a matter of family history, Mother! Besides, aren't you tired of living in a house where everything fragile must be kept four feet off the floor for fear the dogs will destroy it?"

Frank was staring at Louisa again, but she turned her back on him and pointed to her mother's wheelchair. "These days," she went on, "you can't reach things set that high."

Rebecca's eyes narrowed. "I'm not spending the rest of my life in this contraption. And I'm sick of your turning everything into an excuse for railing at my hounds."

Louisa's voice rose to a high quaver. "You always loved those dogs better than me!"

"You made it easy," Rebecca snapped.

Footsteps approached. Yvonne entered the room and caught sight of the broken fern stand. She bent over the largest piece of porcelain and began caressing it as if she were stroking a brow. "Will there be any of *my* family's heirlooms left by the time I can keep them safe?"

Louisa's hands knotted into fists. She faced her mother. "She was just as much my grandmother as *hers!*"

Yvonne rose dramatically. "Grandmama's things are all *mine*. Father knew better than to leave any of our keepsakes to . . . to upstarts!" She stalked out of the room.

"Well, now, that was nearly a breakthrough," Rebecca told Louisa. "You two almost exchanged words directly. Yvonne seems out of sorts this visit. Perhaps I've been too generous with her trust fund lately. Maybe she needs less money to fuss over."

Irma motioned for her husband and Beth to slip away. "We're in for a doozy this time," she whispered once they were out of Rebecca's earshot.

Irma was right. The ensuing argument traveled down the long hall to pierce the calm of the kitchen as Beth and the Smythes resumed their meal.

"You should sell this place while Harrison's offer is still good," Louisa wailed. "Then we can all move to San Francisco where you can get the medical attention you need."

Rebecca's voice rang louder. "Just where am I supposed to keep my kennels? On the roof of a high-rise?"

"Their howling wouldn't be tolerated there. Besides, Mother, the dogs are hard work. You deserve to retire."

"Retire indeed! I handle and breed dogs from desire, not from economic necessity. You and that husband of yours insist on seeing everything in crass business terms."

"For someone in your condition, those dogs are just plain dangerous—especially that beast Lurgan. He's the reason you're in that wheelchair. This time a fern stand—next time, you! You must at least get rid of him!"

"You know perfectly well he's my chief hope of re-establishing a breeding line. With proper handling, he'll be a champion. Without him, it could take a dozen years to put Malvern Kennels back on top."

"But, Mother, in the city—"

"City, city, city! I'm sick of hearing you harp about moving to the city. If you and Paul are so intent on moving to San Francisco, then do so. Just remember this—you won't be living rent-free there. That husband of yours will have to get a real job instead of playing at investment banking."

Louisa's voice rose to a piercing whine. "But we can't leave you like this! Not now that you're so helpless—"

"Can't leave my money, you mean."

Irma rose and shut the door. "That hits the nail on the head," she murmured as she resumed her seat. Then she caught herself and glanced uneasily at Beth. "Of course," she quickly added, "it's really none of our business."

"It's our business when household valuables are broken," Frank said. "They're our responsibility. This week the fern pot, last week an antique figurine. If I had time to follow a certain person from room to room all day, the breakage would soon stop."

Irma shot him a frown. Arnie tucked two rolls into his jacket pocket and excused himself from the table.

"How long have you worked here?" Beth asked.

"Twenty-five years, come November," Irma said.

Beth made a mental note that the Smythes would not have known her mother. "Why has Malvern Kennels been so uncompetitive these past twenty years?"

Frank shrugged. "Training the dogs—with our help on the footwork—is one thing. Handling them at dog shows is another. Mrs. M got so she couldn't move fast enough to show her dogs. She fired one handler after another, then just stopped showing altogether. For a time she seemed happy enough to keep and train wolfhounds for pleasure."

Irma nodded. "Then a writer—some kind of historian of dog breeding—came to interview her on the decline of the kennels. It made Mrs. M furious to find herself considered a has-been. 'Treated like a relic,' she called it."

Frank chuckled. "If there's one thing that always gets Mrs. M's dander up, it's being treated like a relic."

"Is that why Georgia and Matt don't call her 'Grandmother'?" Beth asked.

Irma looked away. "Some folks might say that's it."

"In all the years you've worked here," Beth continued, "have the dogs caused much damage?"

Frank snorted. "Been *blamed* for it, you mean."

"Less in our first two dozen years all put together," Irma added, "than in these past few months."

Beth persisted. "Does Lurgan get most of the blame?"

Frank nodded. "Unless we prove he was with one of us during the moment in question. That throws her for a loop!"

Beth looked from Frank to Irma. "Her?"

Irma looked uncomfortable. "You mustn't mind us, Eliza. It's just that we like the dogs. We can't believe they would turn so destructive and noisy all at once."

"What do you think the problem is?" Beth asked gently.

Irma sighed. "After what you've just heard out there, it can't come as any surprise to you that Mrs. M's daughter finds all these accidents so—well, so *convenient*."

"At first," Frank said, "Louisa just left fragile things in stupid places."

Irma nodded. "After growing up here with wolfhounds constantly in the house, she *should* know better than to leave a china figurine on a low coffee table. Only heavy items that can't be swept off or tipped over by a tail can be left that close to the floor."

"So we started patrolling the house more frequently," Frank continued, "putting back where they belonged any fragile things we found out of place. For a while that worked, but not recently. I figure that someone got mighty impatient waiting for the wolfhounds to wander by pieces of china balanced on the edge of the coffee table."

Beth's eyes widened. "So you suspect Louisa of doing the actual breaking lately?"

Irma sent her husband a quelling look. "Let's just say that every now and then she may give gravity a little help."

Beth ate in silence, absorbing what she had learned.

She didn't, however, want to leave the Smythes on an uncomfortable note. As she finished her coffee, she told them how well adapted their son was for working with dogs.

Frank beamed proudly, but Irma's smile was short-lived.

"I don't know what Arnie will do," she murmured, "when the kennels close."

"With more training," Beth said, "he could always find work as a handler. He's picking up the basics quickly. If Arnie would be interested, I could arrange for him to spend a month or two working for my firm in San Francisco. That would give him experience with a variety of breeds."

Irma sighed. "I don't know if he'd leave for even that short a time. This is the only home he's ever known."

"I'll talk to him," Beth offered.

The gratitude on Frank's and Irma's faces at first embarrassed Beth, then warmed her heart.

After lunch Beth found Lurgan lounging on the back porch. From directly overhead, the sun unfurled a ribbon of blinding light down the driveway. Beth decided to hunt up her sunglasses, abandoned in the car the day she arrived.

She located the car in the vast and gloomy garage that held four other vehicles. One car's front fender looked recently smashed. Beth wondered if that was what got Georgia in so much trouble with her grandmother.

Beth slid into the front seat of her boss's car. At first she thought nothing of flipping up the sun visor. Then it struck her as odd that she had found it down. Arnie had driven the car last, moving it the night of her arrival. He wouldn't have needed the visor in the dark.

Beth pulled the visor back down. Clipped to it were the car's registration and the proof of insurance that the state required all cars to carry. Both were in the name of Lewis Elliott, the car's owner. Had someone checked the registration? Why would they bother? Beth drew a sharp breath. *Maybe they were checking up on me.*

The registration proved that the car did not belong to an Eliza Elliott. But someone snooping might conclude that a male relative named Lewis Elliott held the title until Eliza paid off a family loan. Still, Beth felt uneasy. Did checking the registration mean that someone suspected that Eliza Elliott was a fraud?

Sunglasses on, Beth headed off with Lurgan at her side. Her chest felt tight. Hiding her true identity was getting to her. She'd always considered herself a miserable liar. Now it seemed just a matter of time before she tripped herself up on this lie. Or was her deception making her oversensitive? Perhaps the visor's position meant nothing.

Yet, if *she* was behaving suspiciously, so was whoever slipped into the car. Beth walked faster and with greater determination. If others were checking up on her, she certainly had the right to check up on them. She would start with the mystery of the disappearing sawhorse.

When she came to the spot where she had left the car that first night, she released Lurgan from the leash. "Come on, fella, pretend you're a bloodhound."

He didn't seem eager to leave her side. To encourage him to explore, Beth began wandering off the roadside herself. Stepping from the ribbon of sunlight on the road and into the forest was like stepping from midday to dusk. She took off the sunglasses.

She walked on a layer of dry twigs and needles so deep, it was like moving across an uneven mattress that made crisp noises with each step she took. Overhead, the redwoods were beautiful, but the world at their feet gave Beth the creeps. Nothing grew there. Dead itself, the redwood duff kept the forest floor dead as well and seemed to suffocate the very earth.

Lurgan began sniffing, idly at first, then with more interest. Suddenly he stopped in his tracks.

Beth went to see what had caught his interest behind a fallen log. There, tipped over and hidden from the view of the driveway, lay a lightweight sawhorse.

I wasn't seeing things! Beth reassured herself. *But why did someone remove the sawhorse after I stopped for it?*

Lurgan lost interest in the sawhorse and came to Beth's side. Expertly he positioned his head beneath her hand, then nudged it up, begging to be petted.

Absently Beth complied. The sawhorse perplexed her. Was it intended to turn people back? Or get them to walk to the house in the dark, as she had done? Surely it wouldn't have stopped a member of the household. If her car hadn't blocked the way that night, Ross probably would have moved the barrier and driven on, watching out for the hoses Frank said Arnie sometimes ran across the road.

But Beth had assumed, as any newcomer might have, that she must not drive past the barrier. That's how she had met the dogs when they weren't supposed to be out roaming. Had whoever blocked the driveway also set the dogs free? Anyone who knew wolfhounds knew they would instinctively pursue whatever ran or moved quickly away from them. And for centuries mastiffs had been bred to guard property at night. If the sawhorse failed to turn back a visitor, the two dogs were the perfect combination for scaring off anyone not familiar with giant breeds.

Yet that eliminated a dog trainer as the plan's target. Still, Beth hadn't heard of anyone else expected to arrive at the house. She shook her head. If a string of logic tied together the circumstances, she couldn't find it.

The sounds of a car's engine coming from the main road brought her back to the present. Lurgan had wandered off, and when she gave him the "come" command, he behaved with typical wolfhound tardiness. Some fanciers of the breed dismissed this trait as "responding with deliberate dignity," but to Beth it was just plain stubbornness.

A pickup appeared. Beth took Lurgan in hand in case he had no sense of danger from cars. The pickup slowed to a stop. Ross was driving. Beth flushed to remember how she had taken him for a medic—and how he had let her go on believing that during her embarrassing hiccup bout.

"I have something to show you," she told him when he offered her a lift to the house.

He parked the pickup and followed her off the side of the road. She pointed out the sawhorse but was disappointed when he didn't seem impressed by its discovery.

"But doesn't it strike you as odd," she began, "that someone couldn't wait until daylight to move it? Why did they hide the sawhorse before you or Arnie could see it?"

"Why would they bother?" he asked.

Beth shook her head in exasperation. "Why do *I* bother! Do you think I dragged this sawhorse out here today just to prove that I wasn't hallucinating the other night?"

"No," he admitted. "That doesn't make sense, either."

"Nothing makes much sense unless someone wanted to turn back another visitor, one who would be terrified by Lurgan and your mastiff in the dark."

"But both dogs are harmless. They didn't scare *you*."

Beth hoped her warm cheeks were not giving her away. She wasn't about to confess her moments of terror before she realized her pursuers were dogs. "They wouldn't seem harmless to someone like that woman in the car accident. She's heard about the wolfhounds here and fears them."

Ross shook his head. "She was simply looking for a scapegoat to blame for her own bad driving. Besides, the dogs might scare someone off at first, but a determined person would just bide her time and come back later."

Beth tensed. Bide *her* time?

"What's the matter?"

Beth spoke slowly. "You said 'bide *her* time.'"

A muscle tightened across his square jaw. "So?"

She lifted her chin. *If he suspects me of something, it's better to find out right here and now what I'm up against. I'm sick of living this lie.*

His eyes locked onto hers. A moment passed in which neither spoke. Beth broke the stalemate. "It's obvious you have someone in mind, someone you're expecting to turn up. Someone who isn't wanted. A woman. Who is she?"

"As a matter of fact," he said, after a long pause, "we are expecting someone. Rather, Louisa is. Rebecca and the rest of us aren't convinced anything will come of it."

"Of what?"

He looked away. "For six months now Rebecca has been receiving threatening letters. Louisa is convinced the sender will appear any time now to carry out those threats."

Beth was surprised. "Threatening letters?"

He looked at her once again. "Yes. From a disgruntled woman claiming to be Rebecca's granddaughter."

The words hit Beth like a huge stone thrown into a pond. Their ripples spread wider and wider, widening her disbelief and despair.

"Who?" she managed at last. She waited for him to say anything to prove that her mind was playing tricks on her and he hadn't spoken the words ringing in her ears.

"A woman claiming to be a granddaughter. Someone named Jenny Orne."

Beth's heart rose to her throat and thudded there. "Jenny!" she cried without thinking. "Jenny wouldn't threaten a fly! Besides, it's physically impossible for her to do such a thing. It's a lie—a horrible, horrible lie!"

His eyes searched hers. "You know this Jenny Orne?"

Beth felt her shock and anger melting into something more dangerous. But it was too late. She couldn't stop herself now. "Of course I know her—she's my sister!"

And then she was sobbing, her face in her hands. Several seconds passed before she realized a wolfhound was licking her elbow in an attempt to comfort her. Then someone else tried to comfort her. Beth found herself drawn into a loose, yet warm, embrace.

Beth found herself telling Ross everything. It came out in a jumble, nothing connected to what came before or after. Yet it all came out—her reasons for not revealing her own identity, Jenny's autism, their mother's silence on the subject of her family.

For Jenny's sake Beth had not allowed herself to cry openly since their mother's death. But Jenny was far away from this place, and Beth was surprised to find how natural it felt to let down her guard with the man who had seemed an antagonistic stranger only moments before. Ross no longer challenged anything she said. He listened, speaking only to urge her tale forward whenever she stalled or seemed on the brink of more tears.

What he must think of me! she chided herself when a tear did fall. *What he thinks doesn't matter,* she quickly amended, *just so everything's finally out in the open.*

On that point, however, Ross disagreed. To her surprise, he counseled her to continue to hide her identity.

"I can't!" she exclaimed. "I'm no good at it. Look at how quickly *you* suspected me. I could tell you did from the very first." She remembered the sun visor in the car. "Were you the one who checked the car's registration?"

He looked startled. "Yes. How did you know?"

She explained about the visor's position.

Ross rolled his eyes. "I make as good a detective as you make an undercover agent."

"That's what I mean. You *knew*—right from the start!"

He smiled broadly. "That's because I had the chance to see you before you had your guard up."

"At the accident, right?" When he nodded, she sighed. "I guessed that. But I couldn't put my finger on why I felt certain your suspicions began there."

Ross nodded. "It was something you said when Dell— the ranger—told you to turn back. You said you had a family matter to attend to."

Beth gave a little groan, remembering.

"Normally I wouldn't have noticed such a thing, but Louisa has had us on the lookout for a mysterious *family* member who sent those threatening letters."

"But it wasn't my sister! Whoever concocted such a scheme doesn't know the first thing about her. Many autistics read and write, but Jenny isn't one of them. She has the intelligence for it, but we could never get her to focus on those skills. She did *not* write those letters!"

"I stand corrected," he said, smiling more softly.

That was the smile that won Beth over completely. *I have an ally,* she told herself, surprised to discover that her heart was beginning to hope for even more.

"Still," Ross continued, "those letters kept us on the lookout for someone who might confront—even hurt— Rebecca."

"But implicating my sister makes no sense!"

He looked thoughtful. "It makes a crazy kind of sense once you consider the type of person established by those letters. The writer comes across as a hostile and disturbed person ready to avenge herself if a hefty portion of the family fortune isn't turned over to her."

Beth's mind raced. "But that would only make Rebecca Malvern all the more determined not to turn over a penny!"

"And what better way to discredit the real Jenny Orne?

Rebecca's fortune is vast. Someone might want to make sure your sister—and you—end up written out of the will."

"*Out* of the will? I doubt that we're even *in* it!"

Ross frowned in concentration. "You might be now. Last month Rebecca called in her attorney to rewrite it."

"I don't understand."

"I'm no lawyer," Ross began, "but I can think of a principle that might apply. There's probably a big difference between being mentioned in a will—even if you're disinherited—and not being mentioned at all. In the latter situation, you and your sister might have a legal case for challenging the will by claiming that you were inadvertently overlooked. But if you are mentioned in the will and dismissed—cut out of any inheritance—the will should be less vulnerable to any challenge."

Beth's eyes widened in astonishment. "But if you're right, then that means someone in the house knows about Jenny—and probably about me too!"

Ross nodded gravely. "All the more reason to hide your identity. If whoever is trying to discredit your sister believes you're ready to clear up the misunderstanding, they might move to keep Rebecca from writing another will."

A tingling chill started at the small of Beth's back, then snaked to her neck.

Ross looked straight at her. "If my theory is correct, then once your identity is widely known, your grandmother could be in danger."

Beth swallowed hard. "What kind of danger?"

"That all depends on whether you believe Rebecca's fall was really an accident."

Beth gasped. "Do you mean someone tried to hurt her?"

"Or worse. Maybe they meant to kill her."

Beth's blood turned to ice.

"And if that is even a remote possibility, then we can't rule out another one." His hands tightened their hold on her. "If you get in the way, they might come after you."

Beth headed for her room at the end of the workday. For the sake of appearance, she had spent the afternoon putting Lurgan and a few other wolfhounds through their paces. Despite the shocks she had faced that day, at least she now had something good to look forward to. It had taken some doing, but she had convinced Ross to take one more person into their confidence—his grandmother, Aunt Jen.

"Unless," she had added, "you think it would be unfair to ask her to pretend that she doesn't know about me."

Ross had chuckled. "Gram will be fine. She always said that the only thing she misses here is community theater and those small character roles she used to land. She'll be happy to play this part—if she can just suppress her joy at finding a long-lost niece."

"Great-niece," Beth corrected him. "I guess that makes you and me some sort of cousins?"

He had given her an odd look, and now, turning the knob of her door, Beth had to admit that adding Ross to her list of cousins brought her no comfort.

She stepped inside the dusk-lit bedroom. A movement near the open window caught her attention. It was only the curtain, dancing to the breeze. Still, it seemed a premonition. On the surface, things looked as she had left them, yet she couldn't shake the feeling something was wrong.

She took a closer look. A few things now struck her as being slightly out of place. *Someone's been here snooping.* She closed the door and leaned against it, her heart beating fast. *What were they looking for?* As coolly as she could manage, she went through her belongings. Nothing seemed to be missing. When she came across the file of correspondence between Barking Up the Wrong Tree and Rebecca Malvern, she went through it. Several letters were now out of chronological order. Luckily they gave nothing away.

Next she saw that her hairbrush lay bristles down on the nightstand. She always left it bristles up. Had someone checked the hairbrush for telltale initials? Beth relaxed. None of her belongings bore initials.

That made her think of what Lewis kept on his key chain. She hunted it up. Sure enough, the initials "LE" were engraved on a battered silver dog whistle attached to the car keys. Some people kept the first dollar they ever earned; Lewis kept the first prize he had won for showing dogs. At least the "E" matched her assumed identity. The whistle could pass for a family keepsake.

Next she groped for her back pocket and found the reassuring lump of her wallet. She had packed it along all day. It held all her identification, including her driver's license with her real name on it. She looked once more around the room. On the dresser lay a gasoline receipt from her journey. A tiny alarm went off in her head.

She had used the company's gasoline credit card once, four hours out of San Francisco. Had she grown careless and signed her own name? She examined the thin sheet. She had signed "E. Elliott," just as Lewis had suggested. Then she remembered something else: She *had* been careless—but not about signing her name. She hadn't paid attention to which gasoline she purchased until it was too late. She had written a note reading, *Lewis: Forgive me!* At the bottom of the paper she had explained, *I put in a half tank of cheap-o, low-octane gas. Blame any knocking on me!*

That note was missing. Who had taken it? Not Ross. He had been off the property before the search of her room had taken place. She had met him on his return. Thus, by the time he got to the house, they had joined forces and he was no longer suspicious of her.

Someone else suspects me. She remembered Ross's warning about what could happen if her identity was known. *But that hinges on whether my grandmother's fall was an accident or a deliberate attempt on her life.*

Beth straightened. She needed to learn more about that fall, but she had to be careful not to ask questions that only deepened the suspicions of whoever had searched her room. She would start with the one person, besides Ross, she fully trusted—Aunt Jen. By now Ross would have finished explaining to his grandmother who the dog trainer was. Would Aunt Jen take the news as well as Ross had?

Beth took a quick shower and dressed in a malachite green dress that set off her auburn hair. She wished she had a necklace to liven up the simple dress. Usually it didn't bother her that she owned little jewelry. It seemed silly to buy fashion accessories for herself when the money could be better spent on tapes of classical music that gave Jenny such joy. Though Jenny couldn't read or write, she could, after listening to a piece once, sit at the piano and play it exactly. An "autistic savant," the doctors called her.

Beth put on the colorful silk scarf Lewis and his wife, Annette, had given her for her last birthday. For gift-giving, Beth always baked cookies, decorated in meticulous detail by Jenny. It was one of the rare activities Beth had found that gained her entrance into Jenny's small, private world. But even the cookie project involved risks. Jenny couldn't bear imperfection, so a rule for ensuring her participation was that any "oops" must be swiftly eaten by Beth to hide the evidence. Beth smiled to think of the fuss Annette and Lewis always made over the basket of cookies from the Orne sisters.

As she walked to Aunt Jen's room, Beth grew nervous. Aunt Jen had been friendly enough to Eliza Elliott, a visitor in her sister's home, but would she approve of her long-lost great-niece or her deception in coming here?

Aunt Jen was not in her room. Disappointed, Beth wandered to the living room. From there came strains of piano music. Used to her sister's flawless renditions, Beth winced at an off-note. The music stopped.

The first thing Beth noticed when she entered the living room was Georgia Carstairs sitting on the couch. She looked up from her fashion magazine and gave Beth a slight nod. Beth smiled back, but Georgia was already fingering her way farther through the glossy pages. Beth glanced at the piano and was surprised to find Aunt Jen sitting before it, rubbing the knuckles of one hand. Aunt Jen's sad expression blossomed into a smile when she noticed Beth.

"Sit here," she said, painfully making room on the piano bench before Beth could stop her.

Beth complied, relieved to have Aunt Jen smiling at her. With Georgia present, Beth had to suppress the words and sentiments that would have tumbled out if she had found Aunt Jen alone. "Do your hands hurt?" she asked hesitantly.

"Hand, singular." Aunt Jen spoke with exaggerated crossness. "The right one had its knuckles overhauled last year. Now the left one's turning on me." Without warning, she winked furtively at Beth.

Beth remembered what Ross said about his grandmother's fondness for community theater. He hadn't mentioned her tendency to overact.

Aunt Jen sighed. "Now I'll have to have surgery on the left hand if I'm to regain skill at the keyboard."

"Aunt Jen was a concert pianist in her youth," Georgia interjected, suppressing a yawn. She spoke loudly and slowly. "Tell Eliza about your years on tour, Aunt Jen."

"I'm not hard of hearing," Aunt Jen whispered. Then she raised her voice to a loud quaver reminiscent of maiden aunts in Victorian melodramas. "After a few years on tour, I met my Al, another penniless musician. We stayed with music until we had to choose between it or a family. The adoption agencies kept passing us over until Alfred could show them he had a 'real job.'"

"Tell her about your awards," Georgia boomed.

Beth couldn't figure it out. As bored as Georgia appeared, she was certainly making an effort to take an interest in Aunt Jen. For her part, Aunt Jen didn't appear to appreciate Georgia's efforts.

Aunt Jen winked at Beth. "If she's interested, she'll have to come see them after dinner."

"It's a date," Beth said, smiling.

Aunt Jen's right hand coaxed a graceful trill from the keys. "Do you play, my dear?"

Beth laughed. "Nothing beyond 'Chopsticks.' My sister is the musician of the family."

It had slipped out before she realized it. Worried, Beth glanced over her shoulder and caught Georgia mid-yawn. Georgia hadn't noticed, or if she had, the mention of Beth's sister meant nothing to her.

"How lovely it is to grow up with a sister!" Aunt Jen sounded genuine this time. "What's your sister's name?"

Beth chose her words with great care, pretending that Aunt Jen had asked something else. "I believe she was named for our mother's favorite aunt."

Aunt Jen's eyes grew moist. Her hand closed over Beth's and squeezed it. "Well, my dear," she said, "let's try 'Chopsticks.' I'll play one-handed and you take the bass. On the count of three. One . . . two . . . three!"

It began as an awkward, thundering rendition, with Aunt Jen coaxing Beth to play even louder. Georgia fluttered past them and out of the room.

"Works every time," Aunt Jen said.

They couldn't talk over the music, but the dreadful duet gave them moments alone, moments to enjoy each other's company and reflect on what that company now meant.

Chapter Six

Rebecca reigned at a full table that night. One place remained temporarily empty. Just as Louisa's silver bell announced dinner, Ross had received a message to phone the hospital to confirm a patient's medication.

"I can't remember when we last gathered like this," Rebecca said. "I can't remember *ever* gathering like this."

Paul Carstairs raised his glass. "Here's to long-overdue reunions," he said, striving to sound amiable.

No one joined him in his toast. Louisa looked uneasy. Yvonne glared at her plate. Matt grimaced at Beth as if to warn, "Here we go."

Rebecca shook her butter knife at her stepdaughter. "Yesterday marks the first time since their awkward adolescence that Yvonne and Louisa have deigned to appear together at my table." She turned to Aunt Jen. "Remember that documentary we saw last week? The one with the vulture and hyena warily feeding off the same carcass?"

Louisa dropped her fork. Her daughter seemed the only one oblivious to the tension. Georgia watched the door expectantly. Her low-cut peach sundress struck Beth as inappropriate for such a chilly coastal night.

Aunt Jen folded her napkin. "I'd rather remember the egret scenes if I am to enjoy my meal." She smiled sweetly at her sister. "If, however, you would prefer to discuss less-appetizing matters, I can always eat in my room."

"Never mind," Rebecca said, looking suddenly contrite.

Beth saw what Aunt Jen meant about holding her own with her sister.

Paul began to renew his toast, then broke off to grimace painfully. "Sciatica!" he cried. "I need to take a turn around the grounds. Sometimes I'll be sitting in a restaurant and the pain becomes so *killing,* I simply must get out to walk, walk, walk it off."

"If you've said that once," Rebecca snapped, "you've said it a thousand times. By all means, walk, walk, walk if that will spare us such talk, talk, talk!"

Beth felt sorry for Paul but had to admit Rebecca had a point about his repeating himself. His refrain seemed word for word what he had said when she first met him.

Georgia flashed a smile over Beth's head just as Ross entered the dining room and took his place at the table.

All at once Beth understood Georgia's ingratiating behavior toward Aunt Jen—and a lot more besides that. *Ross!* Clearly Georgia wanted to get on the good side of his grandmother. A twinge of what she hoped was not jealousy caught Beth off guard. *Why, you've scarcely known him for three days!* she teased herself. *And you've scarcely been on good terms with him for three hours!*

Georgia monopolized Ross in spite of Aunt Jen's efforts to draw them into the general conversation. Georgia always managed to pluck Ross's attention back to another of her rapid-fire quizzes about his interests and plans. Because of Georgia's curiosity, Beth found herself learning more about Ross Trenton than she would have if left on her own. She learned he had just finished his residency at a Los Angeles hospital. Georgia clearly considered the place prestigious, for she didn't hide her dismay at learning Ross had turned down a permanent position there.

"My residency taught me," Ross explained, "that I'm not cut out to work as a staff physician at a large hospital."

"But how can you pass up the income?" Georgia cried.

Ross said nothing, but Beth noticed that the same weary look came into his eyes that she had seen yesterday when he had reflected on how people needed occupations they loved.

"It takes years to build up a *private* practice," Georgia persisted. "Look at all the young physicians who have to start out at clinics or as emergency-room doctors."

"Like Ross is doing here?" Aunt Jen spoke with exaggerated sweetness.

Georgia realized her mistake. "But this is temporary, something he's doing just for fun while he's visiting here!"

"In the past month," Ross said, "I've felt of more real use to patients than I did during my entire residency. Here, I can follow through with people instead of passing them down the conveyor belt of impersonal care."

Matt chuckled. "Not to mention Patient Number One!"

Beth assumed Matt was referring to Ross's grandmother.

Aunt Jen set the record straight. "It's nice that Ross

can lend Rebecca a hand after all her help with his medical schooling. Perhaps others will follow suit one day."

Matt raised his glass. "Certainly, Aunt Jen. Georgie can lead off. Whenever Rebecca wishes, Georgie can instruct her on the most economical way to study painting in Rome, London, Athens, and Paris. I believe the trick is to keep all your efforts on a single canvas."

Georgia giggled.

Her mother was not amused. "And when it's your turn, Matt," Louisa said, "I hope you will show us all how to switch your major a dozen times in as many years."

Matt laughed. "*Touché,* Auntie!"

Yvonne glared at Georgia as if she, not her mother, had spoken. "At least my Matt manages to *pass* his courses."

Beth noticed how Rebecca's eyes glittered. Though she didn't smile, the stern matriarch was clearly pleased by the dissension at her table.

"Children, children!" Aunt Jen cried. "I'm sorry I started this. Please, let's eat in peace."

Paul, who had just returned from his outing, tried to comply. He asked his mother-in-law about a subject Beth was sure he found distasteful—the dogs.

"They are doing well," Rebecca replied. "Lurgan will make the big shows this autumn, after all."

"But, Mother!" Louisa cried. "According to Ross, you'll barely be walking by then."

Rebecca made a gesture of shooing off a fly. She looked pointedly at Beth. "I haven't shown a dog in twenty years. Miss Elliott will be handling Lurgan for me."

Beth tried not to show her surprise. Rebecca seemed to be playing a game of cat and mouse with her family, a game she warned Beth not to give away. Still, Beth wasn't about to agree to what had just been sprung on her. "It's an option," she said noncommittally.

Louisa cast a fearful glance at her husband. "There's not enough time to properly train Lurgan," she quavered. "He's been so unpredictable and strange lately!"

After dinner Beth once again gave Aunt Jen an arm to her room. Ross's arm hadn't been available; Georgia had seen to that. She had looped her own through his and asked him to take a look at "a stitch" in her ankle. Beth was happy enough to have Aunt Jen to herself at last. No sooner had they closed themselves inside Aunt Jen's room than they shared a hug.

Aunt Jen laughed through her tears. "I thought that infernal meal would never end! You don't know how badly I wanted to find your mother—but I couldn't get a word out of Rebecca about Helen after their blowup. Well, that's water under the bridge. The important thing now is that I've found *you*—and from what you said earlier, I have another grand-niece in the bargain! Now, tell me everything about you and your sister!"

Aunt Jen shook her head sadly as Beth's tale ended. "Rebecca said she had received news that Helen had died, but she refused to discuss it further. I've never been able to fathom my sister's dealings with her children."

Beth helped Aunt Jen settle into her armchair. "What was it," she asked her, "that drove my mother away?"

"You mean you don't know about—" Aunt Jen broke off to study Beth's face. "You *don't* know, do you?" She made several false starts, then sighed. "There's no easy way to put this. I love my sister, but I'm the first to admit there's never been a woman as obstinate or vain. In a sense, those traits drove your mother off.''

"But why didn't Mom and Rebecca make up eventually?''

Aunt Jen sighed. "With your grandmother, there's no compromise. Once she gives an ultimatum, she can't bring herself to retract it. Your mother was told that if she married your father, she would never be welcome here again.''

Beth couldn't believe what she was hearing. "Their marriage? How could that be the basis of so much ill will?''

"I believe Rebecca relented but was incapable of making the first move. She's suffered for it, your grandmother has. Believe it or not, your mother was her favorite. From what you've told me of your childhood, your mother was a happy woman. Rebecca ended up punishing herself far more than she hurt Helen.''

Beth shook her head. "I still don't understand.''

"This is the tricky part to explain,'' Aunt Jen continued. "I guess you could say it started in our childhood. Our parents scarcely had two beans to cook together. Rebecca's pride couldn't stomach the snubs our poverty attracted—never from good folks, mind you! She especially bridled at the snobbery of the biggest landowners in these parts, the Malverns. When George's first wife died, Rebecca set her cap for him.''

Beth looked away. "She married him for his money?''

"More for the power his money could buy. But she got something she didn't bargain for: Yvonne was only seven but already spoiled and full of prejudice toward my sister. Rebecca lacked the patience to win over her stepdaughter. She packed her off to boarding school instead.''

"Didn't Yvonne ever live here again?"

"No. She remained at boarding school and vacationed chiefly with her mother's family. By the time Yvonne was grown, she and Rebecca were so estranged that my sister built a guest house beyond the kennels chiefly for Yvonne's visits. That's where Yvonne drew the line, however. She refused to be ousted from her family home and always stays under this roof, regardless of the tension."

Beth pictured her mother, Louisa, and Yvonne as girls. She thought of the way Yvonne had mourned the broken fern stand. "Poor Yvonne, she must have felt that Mom and Louisa were invaders taking over and ruining her lovely things. How she must have resented her father's second marriage!"

"Well," Aunt Jen said, "that marriage was no picnic for Rebecca, either. George Malvern was a cranky old coot who thought only of his own comfort. He had every opportunity to do more for Yvonne." She sighed once again. "I'm only telling you these unhappy things so you can understand what came over your grandmother in her early widowhood. That's when she got it into her head she'd been given a second chance at life—and a first chance at real romance.

"It began when she had to call in someone to treat a dog. Your mother was eighteen, I believe. Paul and Louisa were recently married and already living here." She rolled her eyes. "Even then Paul was always on the verge of a big business deal and supposedly 'visiting' here only until his ship came in. I believe that ship must be the *Titanic*."

Aunt Jen seemed reluctant to go on. Beth took her hand and pressed it to encourage her.

Aunt Jen continued. "The professional your grand-mother called in was younger than she. Maybe after being married to a man old enough to be her father, Rebecca thought it was time to average things out in the other direction. The age difference didn't bother her. It was only eight years. Besides, her vanity wouldn't let her face the fact she was no spring chicken. It still won't."

"The man," Beth said, "he jilted her?"

Aunt Jen looked startled. "No! Well, not exactly. But Rebecca did read too much into his visits—especially when he kept dropping by after his veterinarian services were no longer needed." She was studying Beth with a mixture of dread and pity. "What I'm trying to tell you, my dear, is that Rebecca's vanity never recovered from the blow dealt her when the topic of marriage finally arose . . . and she discovered she wasn't the object of it."

Beth's mind spun. Veterinarian services? Slowly the pieces of the puzzle began fitting themselves together.

"You can imagine," Aunt Jen continued, "how crushed my sister was to discover that this man had no intention of courting her. The whole time that Rebecca's vanity coaxed her into believing that he came calling on *her,* he was actually falling in love with her younger daughter."

"With my mother," Beth murmured. Memories surfaced, memories of her mother and father, sharing their happiness. Beth felt one heaviness lift from her heart and another take its place. An old, painful question was gone. But now she must get used to the hard answer filling its void. Now she understood what had driven her mother from her family. *Must it keep Jenny and me estranged from them as well?* she wondered.

Beth scarcely noticed the knock on the door. She was seated on the rug next to Aunt Jen's armchair, imagining a past in which her father visited this house, oblivious to Rebecca's awkward flirtation. The image was grotesque, for Beth kept picturing the father of her youth with her grandmother of the present day. She knew that wasn't right. Back then her father would have been in his mid-thirties and Rebecca Malvern scarcely in her forties.

An unexpected feeling swept through Beth—pity. Pity for the woman who discovered that her daughter was loved by the man she had dreamed of marrying herself. Beth recalled Frank's words, ''If there's one thing that could always get Mrs. M's dander up, it was being treated like a relic.''

A tall figure hovered over Beth. She had not noticed him enter the room and was surprised to find Ross there. She opened her mouth but found no words to express how she felt about all she had learned.

Aunt Jen patted her hand and released it. ''It's a lot to absorb—all this ancient family history. And we can't do a thing to change it. The present's another matter, however. We can work on the present to alter the course of the future. And our immediate concern must be the physical and emotional safety of your grandmother.''

Beth managed a vague nod. She felt numb and far away.

Ross took over. ''When Rebecca was released from the hospital, Gram came here to keep her company. She suspected right off that Rebecca's fall wasn't an accident. Until recently I haven't been easy to convince—''

''But it's better to err on the side of caution than neglect,'' Aunt Jen interjected. ''I'm afraid we haven't narrowed things much. The only people currently in the house who were *not* here the night of the accident are Yvonne, Matt, Ross, myself, and you.''

Ross frowned thoughtfully. ''But we can't rule out the possibility that one of those people was lurking about on that day, out of sight, and intending to do Rebecca harm.''

Beth attempted to wrench herself from the past to the present. ''Who have you eliminated as suspects?'' she asked.

Aunt Jen counted off three fingers. ''The Smythes. First, they're good people. Second, they're afraid of change. If anything happens to Rebecca, their lives would be disrupted at a time when Frank and Irma are too young to retire but feel too old to start over somewhere else.''

Ross nodded. ''Arnie doesn't want things to change, either. Gram's right. All three Smythes would prefer to see Rebecca alive and running the kennels forever.''

''No one's asked about *my* whereabouts that night,'' Aunt Jen said testily. ''I was twelve hundred miles away, playing Mrs. Malaprop in what a local theater critic called 'a miserable attempt to render Sheridan's classic comedy into the modern idiom.' The nerve of that hack!''

Ross nodded sympathetically. ''And I was serving as best man in B. J. Bassett's wedding.''

Aunt Jen squinted at him in mock severity. ''You'd better be able to prove it, young man, if you're to establish an alibi for missing my opening night!''

Ross put his hand over his heart. ''I'll have an eight-by-ten glossy of the wedding party in your hands by Monday.''

Aunt Jen shook a finger at him. ''And how will I know it isn't from *another* of your stints as best man?'' She gave an exaggerated sigh. "Always an usher, never a bridegroom."

Beth was wondering how they could joke about something as serious as attempted murder. Now she began to suspect they were doing it for her sake, to cheer her up. "My sister and I can vouch for each other any given evening," she said, striving to get into the spirit of things. "And my job gives me plenty of witnesses for weekdays."

When she saw the look of relief Aunt Jen cast Ross, Beth knew her hunch had been right. "Seriously," she continued, "shouldn't we question those who witnessed the fall? Louisa said her daughter and husband were present."

Ross nodded. "I tried to grill Paul without letting on that I suspected foul play. He says he heard the sounds of Rebecca's fall from the room next door. He claims he appeared at one end of the stairs just as his daughter showed up at the other. Like his wife, he blames the dog."

"Which end of the stairs?" Beth asked.

"Good point," Ross murmured. "Surely I asked him that—but Paul kept drifting back to Rebecca's position at the foot of the stairs. He seemed convinced that I needed to know which way the hip had twisted so I could treat her accordingly. That information was meaningless, of course, to anyone other than the first doctor to treat her."

"Maybe that was his way of avoiding answering your other questions," Aunt Jen said. "We need to know who was at the *top* of the stairs. Rebecca's no help. Her head took such a crack that the whole week before her fall is a blur."

"What have you learned from Georgia?" Beth asked.

"Yes," Aunt Jen chimed in, wrinkling her nose at her grandson. "What has your newest 'patient' told you about Rebecca's fall? A 'stitch' in her ankle, indeed! In my day we could come up with better ailments than that!"

Ross shrugged. "She had cleared out of here by the time I arrived. But now that she's back, Beth—" He winced. "*Eliza* and I can hear Georgia's version during the picnic Georgia and Matt are planning for tomorrow evening."

Beth nodded absently. Suddenly she understood why she had been invited along. When Matt suggested the picnic, he was helping his cousin, creating an opportunity for her to get away from another horrid Malvern dinner, where romance could only die on the vine instead of blooming. Matt was thinking of Georgia and Ross when he said he didn't want to "play *third* wheel on Georgie's bicycle."

Aunt Jen straightened. "I guess that leaves me to protect Rebecca tomorrow night."

Ross settled himself on the edge of her bed. "You'll have help. I'll ask the Smythes to keep close tabs on Rebecca. But that's all I'll tell them."

Aunt Jen looked from Ross to Beth. "Shouldn't we tell the Smythes our suspicions?"

"We don't want them eyeing people oddly and perhaps tipping them off," Ross said.

"From what I've heard, they already have suspicions of their own," Beth offered. She explained the Smythes' theory about Louisa and all the recent breakage.

"That had better not include a broken hip!" Aunt Jen cried.

The three of them exchanged sober looks.

"We mustn't take any chances with Rebecca's safety," Beth said. "It makes the most sense for me to stay behind tomorrow. I'll say I need the time to work with Lurgan."

Ross looked thoughtful. "But our absence—including yours—could be just what it takes to smoke out Rebecca's enemy. I've met a deputy sheriff on several medical emergencies. Maybe I could talk to him and see what he thinks about keeping an eye on the place. The last thing the local law enforcement wants is to have something suspicious happen to one of their biggest property owners."

Aunt Jen urged him to phone his friend right away.

Ross shook his head. "There are far too many telephone extensions in this house. Sometimes when the hospital calls, I'm positive someone is listening in. No, I'd better drive over there in the morning."

His suspicion about telephone spying reminded Beth of what had happened to her that day. She told them about the search of her room.

Aunt Jen gasped. Ross looked concerned. He suggested that Beth stay in town until the crisis was over.

Beth met Ross's gaze evenly. "I can take care of myself. The more of us here, the safer Rebecca will be."

"You're certainly as stubborn as your grandmother," he said, managing a smile.

"Then it's business as usual until tomorrow night!" Aunt Jen cried, sticking out a fist.

"Business as usual," Beth echoed, laying her hand on top of Aunt Jen's.

"You're outvoted, Ross," Aunt Jen teased.

"All right," he said, placing his hand on top of the pile. "Business as usual." His fingers curved around and lightly caressed the tip of Beth's ring finger.

She looked up and found his eyes holding hers with startling intensity. *Bright smoke,* she thought unaccountably. Then she remembered the dream that had given her that strange phrase. *Where there's smoke,* her heart began telegraphing, *isn't there supposed to be fire?*

For Beth, the "business as usual" bargain didn't last the night. Since Aunt Jen and Ross were anxious for her safety, she didn't say anything to them about the plan that had been forming in the back of her mind all day, a plan to spend the night near the kennels. She was determined to solve the mystery of Lurgan's midnight howling.

That evening, however, sneaking out of the house unobserved proved more difficult than Beth imagined. When she saw that she had to pass the room where Matt, his mother, and Georgia played cards by the open door, she stopped. They might ask why she was bundled up to go outdoors. She returned to her room and stuffed her cap and down jacket into her duffel bag. She hoped they would think she was readying her gear for the next day's work.

Matt made it even easier. "Ah, laundry night! Room for any extra?" he teased.

"You know perfectly well I had Irma do your wash yesterday," Yvonne said, discarding a four of clubs as easily as she discarded any notice of Beth.

Georgia threw Beth a smile. "Are we on for tomorrow?"

"Sure. Do you have any reading for a laundry-sitting?"

Georgia motioned to a stack of her fashion magazines.

Beth entered and took one from the pile. The magazine

would make them think she planned to stay downstairs until her "laundry" was done. Surely they would turn in by then.

Beth found Frank Smythe sitting on the back porch, watching the stars. She told him what she was up to and asked to borrow a flashlight.

Frank nodded in approval. "We'll keep an ear cocked for anyone entering or leaving the house," he said.

Minutes later Beth groped her way through the forest to the kennels. She didn't want to use Frank's flashlight in case the dark held someone else who waited. With that in mind, she went slowly in order to make as little noise as possible. There was no need to hurry. Except for the evening of her arrival, the howling had never begun before the household had settled down for the night.

She avoided the gravel walk and its telltale *crunch*. The wind whispering through the trees masked the sounds of her feet on the redwood duff. When she reached the clearing separating the forest from the kennels, she found the perfect lookout in an ancient stump that time had hollowed into a roomy semicircle. She groped in the duffel and pulled out her cap and down jacket. Already the air was cold and damp with the promise of heavy dew. She put the flashlight beside her and sat gingerly on the duff carpeting the interior of the stump. Now she must wait.

The duff might look as though it suffocated the life from the ground, she thought, but it certainly made a comfortable mattress to lounge on. She leaned back against the inside of the stump and peered out into the clearing, yawning.

A low, distant moan woke Beth. She opened her eyes and kept from moving. From nearby came the sound of a tinny note drawn out, then a lower note, then a clumsy chord drowned out by a full-voiced howl—from Lurgan, no doubt.

Now Beth knew for certain what she had only suspected before. It was music—if the awkward sounds could be called music—that was responsible for setting off Lurgan. Whether he was reacting from the pain in his sensitive ears or was singing along remained to be seen. Her immediate task was to discover the identity of the midnight musician.

Peering beyond the stump did no good. Tendrils of fog had wrapped around the tree trunks, obscuring them. The clearing was anything but clear. The moon had turned it into spectral bands of gauze. Beth rose to her feet only to discover with dismay that both were fast asleep. She furiously wriggled her toes to bring them back to life. The howling never went on for long. She would have to hurry if she was to catch sight of the midnight musician.

She groped her way easily enough along the stump's wall until she came to the opening. Once outside the stump, she would have to get by on her own two feet. Presently they stung in protest of each step she took.

Lurgan was joined in song by another dog. Together they ended a long howl. When they didn't renew their mournful serenade, a new tinny note stirred the air.

Beth realized the musician must be standing where the gravel path opened onto the clearing. She drew the flashlight from her pocket and willed her feet to find their way even though she couldn't feel the ground beneath them. Luck was with her the first few yards. Then one numbed and stinging foot missed its step, and she sank to her knees.

Twigs snapped and crackled beneath her. A few yards ahead, someone gasped hoarsely. Beth flicked on her flashlight only to find that its beam met another to tangle in the thick fog and weave a blinding tapestry of light.

The other beam broke off. For one instant Beth feared for her life. Then she realized her adversary was the one running off, the one afraid of being caught. She glimpsed the white wedge of a shoe's heel as it streaked after the trail blazed by its owner's flashlight.

She scrambled to her feet and began running. Her quarry had a big head start. Then she heard another gasp, followed by the sound of flailing branches. The other runner recovered but lost some ground. When Beth came to that point in the trail, something small and hard smacked her sharply in the abdomen.

She drew up. Her beam of light caught and held a flash of metal that dangled from a redwood branch. Beth paused long enough to grab what had struck her and to jerk it free.

She renewed the chase. Though still somewhat numb, her feet were finally cooperating, and she was gaining on her quarry by the time they neared the house. Through the thick fog, she made out the back door. The figure she chased passed it and darted around the side of the house.

Beth followed. She turned the corner in time to hear a door softly shut. Then came the unmistakable sound of a bolt being drawn. She was locked out.

She spun and raced for another door. By the time she entered it, however, the only sound in the dark was the thumping of her own heart. Disappointed, Beth sank onto the floor. Her hands went limp. One gave up the flashlight. It rolled across the floor, lighting up the wall as it went.

From her other hand, something fell with a *clunk*. She remembered then what she'd found in the dark. She retrieved the flashlight and found her booty. Tied to a length of embroidered ribbon was the source of Lurgan's midnight inspiration. Beth turned it over in her hand. It was a battered children's toy—a tiny harmonica.

She took a deep breath. She had solved the "what" of the mystery of Lurgan's howling. The trick now was to uncover the "who."

Chapter Seven

By morning Beth had a plan. On her way to find Arnie, she heard voices in Aunt Jen's room and knocked on the door. She was pleased to find Ross breakfasting with his grandmother, for she wanted their cooperation in setting a trap. They were alarmed to learn of her midnight adventure but quickly forgot about admonishing her once she produced the small harmonica.

Aunt Jen looked doubtful. "You're sure this is what sets off poor Lurgan?"

Beth nodded. "Twice before, just before Lurgan howled, I caught strains of what must have been notes from this."

Ross took the harmonica from her and examined it. "Now that you mention it, I once heard something strange when the dog acted up. This could account for it. Who was playing it?"

Beth sighed. "That's the problem." She told them about her ill-fated chase. "But with your help, I'm hoping we can watch people's reactions when I try two things."

Aunt Jen grabbed the harmonica and made a sweeping gesture with it. "First you'll pop this on them!"

Beth smiled. "You'll have to coach me to do it with such dramatic flair! Yes, that's the first step. For the next one, we'll need Lurgan. If we each watch the responses of a couple of people, I think we'll learn something."

"I'll take Paul and Louisa," Aunt Jen said. "I'm more familiar with those two than either of you are."

Ross looked at Beth. "Since you'll have plenty to do making your announcement, I'd better watch two people also. If I take Matt and his mother, can you handle Georgia?"

"Sure. That leaves only two problems. First, we need to do this as soon as possible. The less time we give the harmonica's owner to think up excuses, the better. But how do we explain your presence at breakfast? I take it that the two of you don't usually appear for that meal?"

Aunt Jen shook her head. "Too late a start for us go-getters. Today we'll make an exception, of course."

Ross looked thoughtful. "I think that's what Beth is trying to avoid—our doing anything suspicious or unusual. We don't want to put the guilty party on his or her guard."

"That's easy," Aunt Jen said. "I'll come up with something." She shook a finger at Ross. "But you, young man, must stop calling a certain person Beth. You'd never get back on stage if you slipped up during a performance and called your fellow actors by their real names!"

Ross rolled his eyes.

"What was the second problem, *Eliza?*" Aunt Jen asked.

"Your sister. Once I produce the harmonica, if she takes over, that could ruin our chances to catch—"

"No problem," Aunt Jen interrupted. "Rebecca won't be there. She always takes her breakfast alone."

"Well, captain," Ross said to Beth, "it sounds like

we're ready for action.'' He saluted playfully, but his gaze was serious and penetrating.

Without warning, Beth's heart lost one beat, then found three in swift succession. For a split second she was back in the woods, back in Ross's arms. From that look in his eyes, she could almost believe he was there too.

After Beth arranged for Arnie to sneak Lurgan outside the dining room and to keep him out of sight, she hunted up Frank Smythe in the workshop off the garage. She told Frank what she had discovered last night and asked if he or Irma had noticed who came into the house long after dark.

''We were on the lookout,'' he said. ''I can tell you this much—whoever came in first went into one of two doors at the end of your floor.'' He took the pencil from behind his ear, hunted up a scrap of wood, and drew a floor plan.

Beth watched with increasing excitement. Two doors! That narrowed the search considerably!

Frank pointed to two spots at one end of his sketch. ''The two doors,'' he said, ''to what we call the suites.'' He tapped one spot. ''Louisa and Paul have this suite. They use the extra bedroom for Paul's office. Matt and his mother are over on this side.''

Beth's elation shrank. Frank's observation helped clear only one suspect: Georgia. Even that wasn't certain. ''Could someone else—Georgia, for instance—enter either suite in hopes of throwing us off the track?''

Frank scratched his head. ''It's possible. But she'd have a lot of explaining to do to whoever had those rooms.''

"Yes," Beth said. *Unless they already knew what she was up to.* "Frank, while everyone's at breakfast, would it be possible to slip something into each room?"

He shrugged. "I guess so. That's when Irma makes up all the beds."

"Then here's what I'd like Irma to do. Could she put one of these in plain sight on each bed?" Beth pulled out several strips she had cut from the broken ribbon attached to the harmonica.

Frank looked perplexed. "I can't see any harm in it. It's not like it was a dead snake or something."

"For one person," Beth murmured, "I'm counting on it being just that."

At the family breakfast, Aunt Jen moved her food around on her plate so expertly that anyone who didn't know she had already eaten would never have guessed that she was anything but famished. Beth was intentionally late for the meal. When she arrived, she could see that Aunt Jen must have successfully explained away Ross's presence and her own.

Beth ate absently, listening for the signal to begin her plan. At last she heard the telltale *clicks* of Lurgan's nails across the polished floor next door. She was relieved that no one else seemed to notice.

Aunt Jen caught Beth's slight nod and began. "And tell us, Eliza, how's the training going?"

"Fine," Beth said, remembering to watch Georgia's reactions. "For one thing, we can all rest easier now that one problem has been solved." She paused for emphasis. "Here's the answer." Then she held up the harmonica so that everyone could see it. She watched Georgia squint slightly and bend forward. She looked genuinely puzzled.

''Why, that's mine!''

It was Matt who spoke up. He surprised Beth by stretching across the table and taking the tiny instrument.

He examined it. ''Remember this, Georgie? Rebecca took it away. See those dents? They're from your teeth before you understood the concept of playing a harmonica.'' He held it closer to his cousin. ''Look at how uneven that row of dents is—it's a good thing you eventually got braces!''

Georgia initially looked insulted, then seemed infected by her cousin's good humor. She elbowed him playfully in the ribs. ''At least I *had* front teeth that summer!''

Beth reached for the harmonica, but Matt didn't seem to notice. Before she could stop him, he raised it to his lips and played a soft riff.

''A couple of reeds are out of commission,'' he said. He licked his lips and blew a loud, long chord.

Beth's heart sank. She had intended to have Arnie bring Lurgan into the room before she demonstrated how the dog responded to the harmonica. That way the guilty party would expect something the others wouldn't and would react differently. But now it was too late. From the next room, Lurgan gave a preliminary whimper and then began howling.

Thus everyone was equally caught by surprise. Yvonne and Paul gasped in concert. Louisa dropped her spoon. Even Ross looked startled by the volume of the sound. Matt and Georgia gaped at each other before bursting into laughter.

Beth was thankful she had one more card up her sleeve. ''Mrs. Malvern charged me with discovering what caused Lurgan's nightly serenading. I'll show her the harmonica,

of course.'' She looked slowly from face to face.
''Whether she needs to know *all* I have discovered depends on how satisfactory an explanation I receive.'' She
gestured for the harmonica's return. ''If I hear nothing
by lunch, I'll assume Mrs. Malvern should be told everything.''

''That sounds like a fishing expedition,'' Matt said.

Beth strove to look self-assured. ''No. The person who
needs to see me will get a private signal.'' With that she
rose and turned from the table.

No one spoke. In that moment Beth understood the
terrible power Rebecca Malvern must feel when she manipulated her dependents. *But this is for a good cause,*
Beth tried to tell herself. *I'm not like her. I'm not.*

Beth lingered in her room for half an hour, hoping for
a knock on the door. When none came, she tried imagining how the guilty person must be feeling. She decided
that no one would want to knock on a door that others
might be peeking at. The kennels would be a better place
to wait.

She put a dog whistle around her neck and went downstairs, making more noise than usual. She found Lurgan
lounging in the empty kitchen and took him along. Even
though the day was bright and sunny, she didn't want to
walk the path through the forest alone.

At one point on their journey through the cool, dark
woods, Lurgan padded ahead of her, out of sight. Beth
used the dog whistle. She couldn't hear it, but she knew
the wolfhound could. She was pleased to see that he came
bounding back into sight, alert and ready for further
orders. Rebecca had obviously trained him to respond
to it.

She was relieved when they stepped into the clearing separating the path from the stretch of kennels. She preferred open ground. Ahead, however, she saw that the door to the kennel storage room stood ajar. She took a steadying breath. Arnie would never leave the door open, especially not overnight. Marauding raccoons would get into the kibble. Either Arnie was in the storage room that instant, or someone else was there, waiting.

Beth gathered Lurgan into the heel position and attached the tab leash to his collar. Together they went to the door. When she stopped, the wolfhound automatically sat at her side. Beth listened a moment but heard nothing. She braced herself. "Come out," she said.

The door opened a bit farther.

"You come in," came a whisper so hoarse that it could belong to either sex. "I don't want to be seen."

Lurgan whimpered slightly. Beth could remember him reacting that way to only one person. "I'm staying where I am," she said. "Say what you've come to say, Louisa."

The door opened fully. Louisa Carstairs stood there trembling. In her hand she clutched a length of pink, embroidered ribbon that Beth had removed from the harmonica.

Beth silently thanked Irma and fleetingly wondered what the others had made of the scraps of ribbon on their beds.

"Does anyone else know?" Louisa's voice quavered.

Beth didn't want to appear as though she acted alone. "Yes, but never mind about that."

"I didn't mean any harm," Louisa whined. "I only wanted to help Mother realize that the dogs have become more than she can handle. She's too frail—they're a danger to her. I'd never forgive myself if she got hurt again and I hadn't tried to get her out of harm's way!'' She buried her face into her hands and began sobbing.

Beth entered the storage room. A breeze nearly closed the door behind her. She felt sorry for Louisa and let her finish crying and regain her composure. Louisa's collar had come open to reveal an ugly red welt across her neck. Beth realized it could have happened last night when the harmonica's ribbon caught on the branch. She recalled the way Louisa had toyed with her collar the first evening. She'd been making sure the harmonica was hidden from sight.

''It's not just the dogs,'' Louisa said at last. ''I've got to get her out of here—there's no time to lose! If we lived in a high-rise apartment—the kind with an elaborate security system and guards on duty—Mother would be safe from the crazy woman after her. We can't protect her here, out in the middle of nowhere.''

Beth's sympathy dissolved into anger. *She means Jenny!* ''You'd better explain,'' she said stiffly.

Louisa waved the scrap of ribbon. ''Threats! Terrible letters demanding money—or else. I wanted to turn them over to a detective agency.''

A breeze almost closed the door as Beth's mind whirled. Any half-competent investigator could expose the letters as a fraud. The forger would know that. If Louisa wanted to call in a detective, she had to be innocent of the hoax.

''So, you see,'' Louisa continued, ''I thought that if Mother could be convinced that the dogs were too unruly, she might give up the kennels and move to safety.''

Beth felt Louisa was sincerely concerned for her mother's security. Yet what the Smythes said was probably true also—Louisa would welcome the chance to leave this isolated spot and move to the city. Lurgan nosed the door back open. This time Louisa didn't cringe at the sight of him in her usual way. Clearly that had been an act to underscore her claim that the dog was dangerous.

"The night I arrived," Beth said suddenly, "you were the one who let the dogs out, weren't you?"

Louisa nodded. "I hoped that if that crazy woman was lurking about, the dogs would alert us—or give her a good scare. When I was sure they were after something, I decided Lurgan's howling might frighten off whoever was out there."

"And the sawhorse? That was meant to increase the distance a newcomer would have to walk?"

Louisa nodded again. "And give the dogs a better chance of noticing her approach. I had forgotten that was the day you were to arrive. When you turned out to be the trainer—well, I was afraid you'd heard the harmonica and would explain away Lurgan's behavior to Mother."

Beth straightened. "Then *you* were the one who moved the sawhorse?"

"It was all I could think of," Louisa whined, "to confuse matters. I knew you'd mention it. I hoped that if people believed you were wrong about that, they'd think you were wrong about hearing music as well." She looked pleadingly at Beth. "Are you going to tell Mother about my part in the . . . in the way Lurgan's been acting?"

Beth considered the situation. "I won't have to." She watched as relief, then something too close to triumph, lit Louisa's eyes. "Because you're going to do it."

Louisa's mouth dropped open. "I—I can't!"

Beth shook her head. "You can and you must. From what I've seen of your mother, she has her suspicions already." She spoke more gently. "Wouldn't you rather tell her yourself than have her hear it from someone else?"

Louisa's expression of alarm hardened into a frown. "Yvonne!" she hissed. "She'd just love to tell Mother! I saw how she kept an eye on your door after breakfast!"

Beth felt heavyhearted. The vulnerable Louisa had vanished; the bitter, jealous Louisa was back in her place. There was nothing more to say. Beth left the storeroom. She knew who was stirring up Lurgan at night, but had she come any closer to learning who was threatening Rebecca?

Beth spent an uneventful two hours working with Arnie and the wolfhounds. The dogs gave them so little trouble that she doubted whether Arnie was learning anything new. Afterward she barely touched her lunch with the Smythes. She simply wanted it to end so that she could meet with Ross and Aunt Jen as planned.

Maybe they could make more of Louisa's confession than she had been able to do. If Louisa was telling the truth, or simply telling the truth as she saw it, then Rebecca's enemy was no closer to being exposed than before. Beth was glad this was Ross's day off—and not only, she was beginning to realize, because she wanted his opinion.

Now that her early misunderstandings with Ross had been cleared up, she could feel something else taking their place, something that had eluded her—or that she had eluded—since taking on sole responsibility for Jenny. She wondered if Ross felt anything for her.

After lunch, Beth was halfway down the hall when she heard faint screams coming from the far end of the house. She ran in their direction, turning a corner and starting down the long hall toward the bedrooms. Heading straight for her was Aunt Jen, limping with as much haste as she could manage.

"Go back!" the older woman shrieked. "The pond! I saw it through my window! The pond!"

Beth spun on her heel and raced through the sitting room, straight for the double doors leading outside onto Rebecca's forbidden sanctuary, the new deck overlooking the wide, shallow pond. Pulling open those doors forced Beth to pause just long enough to engrave forever in her memory the scene outside.

The unfinished deck jutted over the pond less than a foot above its surface. In the middle stood Lurgan, his legs completely immersed, his back arched above the surface. His massive head was bent forward and down, his nose only inches from the water. Two gaunt arms circled his neck.

In that instant it seemed to Beth as though those pale arms belonged to an ancient water spirit tugging the dog to a cold, dark death. The wolfhound braced with all his might against the pull yet did nothing to break free from it.

A few feet from the dog, shining stripes and curves wavered in the water. Beth saw through the distortion of the surface and was able to make out metal bars and a large thin-rimmed wheel. Suddenly she realized what she was seeing—Rebecca's wheelchair. Beth's mind regis-

tered one more thought: *My grandmother is drowning!*
Then thought fled her as she bolted to the deck's edge
and jumped.

The water reached halfway up Beth's thighs. She
moved as fast as she could. Still, it was like moving
through wet cement, fighting for each step but making
little progress.

Now she could see her grandmother's head pressed
against the dog's neck, her arms circling his back. Facedown, her nose barely out of the water, Rebecca sputtered
for breath. The overturned wheelchair held her legs fast.
She had been unable to free herself to stand or even to
kneel in the shallow water.

Beth's mind reeled. Lurgan—and the strength of her
arms—kept Rebecca from drowning. What if he—or
they—had given out before someone came?

Gingerly she freed Rebecca's legs, praying she was
not further complicating any unseen injuries. Next, Beth
gripped her around the waist and kept her afloat as she
guided her toward the water's far edge. The deck was
closer, but to avoid twisting Rebecca's body, Beth moved
the invalid in the direction she already faced.

On the opposite side of his mistress, Lurgan seemed
to understand what was needed of him. He moved slowly
and steadily, Rebecca still clutching his neck. As soon
as they reached the pond's edge, Rebecca released Lurgan
and grabbed for a massive stone bordering the water. Her
other arm snaked around Beth.

Beth gasped with shock and pain as that hand dug into
her flesh. In her grandmother's grasp she felt a determination to cling to life, whatever the cost.

Rebecca was blinking furiously. Suddenly her eyes

focused on Beth. In a cross between a cry of recognition and one of accusation, she uttered a single word: "You!"

The first person to reach them was Matt. "Rebecca," he urged, "take my hand."

Rebecca only intensified her grasp both on the rock and on Beth.

In a jumble of alarm and confusion, the rest of the household assembled at the pond's edge. Aunt Jen's pale and stricken face appeared next to the shocked ones of Yvonne and Louisa. It was Ross who splashed into the water and gently but firmly disengaged Rebecca's arm from around Beth. He gave directions to those hovering at the pond's edge.

"Irma, call an ambulance and bring my medical bag."

Georgia was clutching her neck and making mewling noises. Ross asked her to gather blankets. He told the men to move enough of the rocks bordering the pond to clear a space to lay Rebecca down. Frank and Arnie did as asked.

"The deck is flat already," Matt protested.

"But too high for us to lift her safely," Ross replied.

Matt nodded and set to work. When the space was cleared, Arnie joined Beth and Ross in the pond to lift Rebecca. Frank and Matt remained on dry ground to help. Gently Beth and the four men eased the injured woman out of the water.

It was only then that Beth saw what was looped around her grandmother's wrist—a leather dog leash.

Absently Beth sought the submerged end of the leash and held it up. Something was wrong. The leather loop gaped open, its heavy stitches severed. The bridle snap for attaching the leash to a dog's collar was missing.

Yvonne gasped and stared at what Beth held. Seconds later Louisa let out a cry and pointed an accusing finger at Lurgan. Everyone stared at the wolfhound. Lurgan stood nearby in the water as though waiting for a command. Head held high, eyes alert, he panted from his recent exertion.

Then Beth saw it. Dangling from the dog's collar was the leash's missing bridle snap.

Louisa continued to point at it. "That beast! He did this! He nearly killed Mother again!"

Beth was quick to react. "Lurgan saved her life. He kept her head above the water. Without him, she would have drowned instantly."

Paul Carstairs spoke from the outer fringe of the faces. "Without him, she would never have been dragged into the water in the first place. It's clear that he bolted after something—a bird, perhaps—and dragged his hapless mistress after him."

Rebecca began a snarl that turned into a hacking cough.

"Don't talk," Ross ordered her. "Save your breath."

"She's taken on some water," Aunt Jen quavered.

Ross nodded. "But not enough to need CPR and risk having her ribs cracked—if they're not that already."

Georgia returned with a flimsy, ruffled bedspread. Ross frowned but accepted it. He wadded it into a pillow and placed it beneath his great-aunt's head. He nodded approvingly at the heavy blankets Irma produced along with his medical bag.

Rebecca lay waist-level to him. He remained in the pond to examine her. When he finished, he wrapped the heavy blankets around her, tucking them gently under her good hip. "How long before the ambulance gets here?" he asked.

Rebecca sputtered something that lost itself in a watery cough.

Ross seemed to understand her. His hand folded over hers. "You must go to the hospital. Not only for X rays but also to make sure your lungs are clear and stay that way. Doctor's orders," he added, forcing a smile. Then he turned to Irma. "The ambulance?"

Irma looked anxious. "I started to call for one, but then I remembered that special medical-emergency vehicle on display up at the ranger substation this week."

Ross's eyes widened. "That's just to win over taxpayers to the idea. It's fully equipped but isn't staffed for real service."

Worry creased Irma's brow deeper. "Last time, the ambulance took over an hour just to get here. I figured the mobile unit was a lot closer. I guess *they* figured that you could staff it. Once I mentioned your name, they seemed eager enough to give it a go."

Just then the first shrieks of a distant siren pierced the air.

Ross looked suddenly convinced. "Good thinking, Irma."

Most of the household left to meet the siren and flashing lights. Louisa stayed behind to fuss over her mother's blankets. Rebecca blinked repeatedly at the sky.

Ross studied her eyes. "You're not in shock. Have you taken any medication recently?"

Rebecca's hand rose in an angry gesture that set her coughing again.

"Never mind," Ross said.

Arnie began to lift the wheelchair out of the water.

"Hold on a minute," Beth said, wading over to help

him. "Try not to disturb anything as we lift it. I need to check something." She took hold of the wheel's push rim. The cold had caught up with her. She shivered uncontrollably as they raised the chair out of the water.

"Just as I thought," she murmured before turning back to Rebecca. "Don't talk," she told her. "Just nod or shake your head. Did you remember to set the wheel lock?"

Rebecca's nod was a forceful and irritated affirmative.

Ross looked thoughtful. "Yes, of course she would."

A different chill now shook Beth. *But the wheel lock wasn't set. Either she's mistaken—or someone unlocked it!*

A woman appeared with a folded stretcher. "I guess I'm your driver," she announced to Ross. "I never expected to do anything more than display this rig."

Ross oversaw the transfer of Rebecca onto the stretcher. Once she was safely on her way to the emergency vehicle, he turned his attention to Beth. She struggled out of the pond, her feet too numb to register solid footing.

"You're shivering," he said.

But Matt reached her before Ross could. Quickly Matt caught up a damp blanket abandoned when Rebecca was wrapped in the ones that came with the stretcher. He swept the blanket around Beth's shoulders. Nothing remained for Ross to do but offer Arnie the other blanket and help him coax the wolfhound back onto land.

The driver returned for Ross. Louisa insisted on accompanying Ross and her mother for the hour's ride to the hospital. But it was Beth to whom Rebecca beckoned before the emergency vehicle carried her away.

The hand gripping Beth's arm held on like an eagle's claw clutching a precarious perch. "Save the dog," she commanded in a voice hoarse from coughing. "Save them all."

"I will," Beth promised. But when she tried to pat Rebecca's hand in a gesture of comfort, the old woman waved her off angrily.

Before the driver closed the vehicle's huge doors, Beth had only a fraction of a moment to exchange glances with Ross. She knew hers was a look of confusion and exhaustion.

But Ross's eyes held a different message. *Be careful,* they seemed to say

When the lights disappeared down the driveway and into the forest, the full import of Ross's unspoken warning hit Beth. *This was no accident! Whoever tried to make it appear like one will surely try again to . . . to kill.*

Chapter Eight

 " "You have no say in this—no say
whatsoever!" Louisa fumed at
Beth over the telephone. "That dog *will* be put down—
and that's the end of it." She hung up.

Beth was left staring in shock at the phone receiver.
Louisa planned to have Lurgan destroyed.

Lurgan lounged at Beth's feet. She stroked his massive
head. "No one will harm you, fella. I promise you—just
as I promised your mistress."

The dog drew the tip of his tongue across Beth's wrist.
She sighed. Promising was one thing; carrying through
was quite another. She needed a plan for keeping Lurgan
safe until his mistress was released from the hospital.
Louisa hadn't said when that would be. Before she had
begun railing against Lurgan, Louisa reported that Rebecca's X rays showed no bones broken. Her lungs were
somewhat congested, however, so the doctors planned to
keep her under observation for a few days.

Beth thought hard. From everything she had observed,
Lurgan was clearly innocent. If Louisa knew that, then
she might have been the one behind Rebecca's latest
mishap. Louisa certainly wanted Lurgan to take the
blame. Even if she wasn't involved in either of Rebecca's
"accidents," Louisa's desire to rid her mother of the

Lurgan safely out of sight until Arnie drove up in his father's truck. As soon as Arnie opened the tailgate, Lurgan jumped onto the bed of the truck and made himself comfortable atop a jumble of camping gear, dog kibble, and ice chests.

"Sorry it took so long," Arnie said. "Mom packed food for a month! Like you, she decided she'd better not know exactly where I'm headed." He reddened slightly. "But I had to promise to find a phone and call her now and then."

"Fine," Beth said. "That way we can let you know when the coast is clear for you to bring Lurgan home."

Arnie nodded gravely. For the first time since Beth had met him, she thought he looked his age.

After seeing Arnie off, Beth tried to slip back to the house without being seen. As she started up the front steps, however, the door opened. Out popped Paul Carstairs.

"I saw you lead the dog away," he said, studying her. "My wife would consider that a serious breach of contract."

Beth's stomach tightened into a queasy knot. *Will Louisa fire me? I could still protect Lurgan—but that would leave one less person to look after Rebecca.*

"Before you say anything," Paul continued, "I must warn you that Louisa has entrusted me with the task of destroying the animal. I tried to plead my sciatica." He paused to touch his hip gingerly. "It's acting up again. Sometimes I'll be sitting in a restaurant and the pain becomes so *killing,* I simply must get out to walk, walk, walk it off."

Beth's mind spun. *If I hear that once more, I'll scream!*

Why is he stalling? It's clear he knows I've done some-thing with Lurgan.

Paul seemed to catch himself. "I didn't mean to go on so. Anyway, my wife was quite hysterical. Before I begin my search in earnest, however, I thought that per-haps if I gave you fair warning—say, one hour?—then I might not be able to find the poor beast."

Beth stared at him in disbelief. "You mean you'd . . . you'd *help* protect Lurgan?"

Paul put a well-manicured hand over his mouth. "I certainly can't go *that* far—not after what happened to-day."

"What happened today is that Lurgan saved your mother-in-law's life!" Beth cried.

Paul waved his hand in a limp gesture of dismissal. "Be that as it may, what concerns me is what is *yet* to happen today. As I see it, my wife will simply blame me for failing to find the dog. I *never* saw you with him, is that understood? That can just remain our little secret. What Louisa doesn't know, won't hurt her."

"Well, then," Beth said in a small, uncertain voice, "thank you."

Paul nodded. "Not at all." He turned and disappeared into the house.

Georgia was clearly disappointed that Ross was staying in town to keep track of Rebecca's progress. Another doctor on duty at the hospital had offered to switch nights with him. The picnic Georgia had planned for that eve-ning was now rescheduled for tomorrow. That, however, did little to mollify Georgia. When Beth suggested that the rest of them go ahead as planned—but without Ross—

Georgia looked as though she had suggested going scuba diving without oxygen tanks.

Another person wasn't coming home that night. Claiming to be exhausted, Louisa was staying in a motel near the hospital. Beth couldn't help wondering if Louisa's plan was to be as far away as possible when Lurgan was supposedly destroyed—as if that would remove her from any blame.

Though the picnic was postponed, Beth wanted to use the evening as originally planned—to probe Georgia's version of how Rebecca broke her hip. Since Georgia was in no mood for visiting, however, Beth decided to question Paul instead.

Paul wasn't in his rooms or in any of the family rooms. It was Irma who set Beth on the right path.

"Since Mrs. M's not around to catch him, he'll be in her den playing king." Irma scowled wryly.

Paul had not shut the door to the den firmly. When Beth tried to knock, she succeeded in pushing the door wide open.

Paul sat at his mother-in-law's desk. Caught off guard, he looked frightened. Then he laughed nervously. "You surprised me with my hand in the cookie jar!"

But what Beth saw glinting in his hand was no cookie. Paul was oiling a gun.

He spoke in a conspiratorial whisper. "I thought I'd better make a good show of it for Louisa's sake—about the dog, I mean. She'll be quite angry when she finds that the deed's not done. If she sees that I readied a gun, perhaps she won't suspect that I looked the other way."

Beth was puzzled to see Paul behaving like a henpecked husband. At the dinner table it was always Louisa who did the cringing. Perhaps she was the timid one until something worked her up enough to turn the tables in the marriage, even if only briefly.

Paul gave the pistol a final buff with a rag, then replaced it in the nearby trophy case. He carefully positioned the gun before he locked the case and slipped the key under the blotter on the desk. "Now, then," he said, "how may I help you?"

Beth took the chair across from him. "As his trainer, I have to get to the bottom of Lurgan's behavior."

Paul looked bored. "Oh, but I thought you resolved all that this morning."

"Yes, the matter of the howling has been put to rest." Beth wondered if Paul knew his wife was the source of that problem. *He must,* she thought. *He was bound to notice how she came and went whenever the dog acted up.*

"It's the other matter I need help with," she continued. "I need to understand Lurgan's behavior when your mother-in-law broke her hip. You witnessed Rebecca's fall, didn't you?"

Paul sighed heavily. "The aftermath will forever live in my memory. The way Rebecca lay there, twisted to one side—"

"It's what preceded her fall that I'm interested in. Where was Lurgan when you first saw him?"

Paul folded the rag he had used to clean the gun, neatly squaring its corners. "He lunged down the stairs and began nosing at her."

"You saw him go down the stairs, then?"

He flicked at something on his cuff. "Anyone could tell by his position over Rebecca that he had come down, not up, the stairs."

"Your wife says that you and your daughter witnessed the actual fall and saw the dog—" She broke off, unwilling to use Louisa's word, "attack." "She said you two saw the dog trip Mrs. Malvern."

Paul nodded vigorously. "Yes, my wife said that."

Beth tried again. "But is her account accurate?"

Paul shook his head slowly. "That was weeks ago. It's grown fuzzy now. I certainly *heard* Rebecca fall. All that dreadful thumping! I tell you, it's a miracle she only broke her hip and not her neck."

"Please help me understand," Beth said, hiding her mounting irritation with his roundabout ways. "Are you saying that you *did* or *did not* see the actual fall?"

Paul sighed. "I'm sorry I can't be of more help."

Beth tried another approach. "Where was Georgia when you first realized she was present?"

Paul looked bewildered. "Isn't it the dog's position at the accident that matters?"

"Of course, but I need to picture the scene clearly if I'm to understand what happened. Now, did Georgia arrive on the scene *before* or *after* you did?"

"Before." Paul shuddered. "Rebecca lay there, so broken, so helpless!"

"And you? Where were you standing?"

Paul closed his eyes and shuddered again. "Where I could see all the horror of it!" Beth took a long breath before continuing. "You were standing nearby, then? Next to your mother-in-law?"

He nodded. "Close by. Too close, I assure you, for me to ever forget—"

"But," Beth persisted, "*where* were you standing in relationship to the stairs?"

He blinked. "Why, I believe I was gripping the railing." He glanced at his watch. "We'll be late for dinner. With Louisa absent, we can't count on her bells."

Beth spoke through clenched teeth. "At the *top* or the *bottom* of the stairs, Mr. Carstairs?"

"Paul—do call me Paul, Eliza."

"At the top or the bottom, *Paul?*"

He looked perplexed. "Why, at the bottom, of course."

Dinner did nothing to relieve Beth's feeling of exhaustion from following the twists and turns of Paul Carstairs's mind. Nor was he ready to drop the subject Beth had reopened for him. During the soup course everyone had to sit through his graphic description of Rebecca's prone body the day she broke her hip. Then he jumped to still another chorus of how his sciatica often drove him away from enjoying hot meals in restaurants.

Afterward Beth and Aunt Jen slipped off to swap notes. Aunt Jen wasn't surprised to learn that Louisa had been the one behind Lurgan's howling. She even sympathized with what she considered Louisa's motive for her actions.

"Don't you see, my dear?" Aunt Jen said. "If Louisa didn't have Lurgan to blame for Rebecca's broken hip, then she might have to wonder if her husband or daughter had anything to do with it. Remember, those two were already there by the time Louisa arrived on the scene."

Beth thought a moment. "So you're suggesting that Louisa's campaign against Lurgan is motivated in part by loyalty to Paul and Georgia? Or by a need to deny the possibility of their involvement?"

Aunt Jen smiled sadly. "Yes, though Louisa may not

consciously realize it. Even your Aunt Louisa has her soft spots.'' She brightened. "But now it's my turn! This afternoon I initiated a game of where-were-you-when-you-*heard*-about-Rebecca's-broken-hip with Yvonne and Matt. From there, I worked them back to discussing where they were when Rebecca actually took the fall.''

Beth looked doubtful. "Didn't they find that an old topic?''

"They weren't at all suspicious," Aunt Jen insisted. "They assume that people my age dote on reminiscing about where they were when Pearl Harbor was bombed or when man first stepped on the moon. Anyway, on the day in question, Yvonne said she was serving as a tour guide for a Sacramento art museum. Later I phoned there, pretending to be a grateful tourist who wanted to thank the 'lovely lady' on duty that day. They checked the schedule and gave me Yvonne's name.''

Beth smiled. "You're good at this detective business, aren't you?''

Aunt Jen's eyes narrowed. "Well, we can't rule out the possibility that Yvonne hired an actress to stand in for her that day to give her an alibi. Still, it's a start.''

"Good work," Beth said. "And Matt?''

"Matt thinks that was the day he appealed a ticket in traffic court in Shasta County. That would place him closer to here, but still several hours away.'' Aunt Jen frowned. "This one is trickier. I called pretending to be an employer checking on Matt's excuse for missing work that day, but the clerk told me I was welcome to come look through the records myself but he couldn't give out such information over the phone.''

Beth offered to drive over there the next day.

Aunt Jen patted her hand. "Maybe I can save you the time. I have an old school chum who retired over that way. I'll try to reach him by phone and see if he'll do the footwork for us."

"I don't know about this telephoning," Beth said. "Ross doesn't think the phones here are all that private."

Aunt Jen rolled her eyes. "We haven't time to sneak out to the nearest pay phone. That's some twenty miles away. Rebecca could be home the day after tomorrow." She looked at Beth solemnly. "We have to figure this out before that happens. After today—" She broke off, turning pale.

It was Beth's turn to pat Aunt Jen's hand. "I know," she murmured. "From the moment Rebecca returns here, her life is in danger."

Chapter Nine

In order not to arouse any suspicion, Beth put in a business-as-usual morning. She worked with the wolfhounds and even enjoyed a surprising breakthrough with Ross's dog, Saxon. When the mastiff came to his gate and whimpered slightly, Beth took that as a sign that he was finally willing to be friends. Once she had him on a leash, she discovered how rudimentary his training was. Yet he seemed happy to be out of his run. Beth decided that this time she should do no more than let him get used to her.

She led him away from the training grounds and soon found herself on an overgrown path cutting through a thick stand of redwoods. When she looked up from swiping a last low branch from her face, she was surprised to find before her a spacious house modeled after the even larger Malvern mansion. She realized this must be the guest cottage Aunt Jen mentioned.

Then Beth remembered why the house had been built—to manipulate Yvonne and keep her at a distance. She shook her head sadly. Its boarded windows betraying years of silence and disuse, the guest house stood for everything wrong with Rebecca Malvern's relationship with her offspring—manipulation, lack of communication, isolation, and boarded-up secrets.

Beth returned for lunch at "the big table," as Arnie called it. She would have preferred eating with Irma and Frank Smythe, but Aunt Jen had convinced her to spend more time with "the suspects," her term for both Sandersons and all three Carstairs.

"The more of *us* present," Aunt Jen had reasoned, "the better chance of noticing when one of *them* slips up."

Beth certainly didn't notice any slip-ups at lunch, however. Matt received a phone call just before he sat down, and he appeared sadly preoccupied throughout the meal. For once Yvonne and Louisa passed up chances to argue with each other through their children. Even Paul was unusually quiet. Beth wondered if those three were angry at one another or if they had struck a secret truce.

Aunt Jen was also quiet. Clearly she was keeping an eye on her five "suspects." As if to explain away her behavior, she said she was feeling stiff. "There must be a change of weather coming," she told no one in particular. "My joints feel this way before the autumn rains start."

"Yes," Louisa said dully, "the barometer is dropping. Rain isn't predicted, but we're in for some unseasonable wind." Then she shot Beth a dark look.

Louisa had arrived home just before lunch, and Beth guessed that Louisa held her responsible for the fact that Lurgan was alive and missing.

Georgia was left to carry the conversation. With Ross present, she appeared eager to do just that. After he cut off her renewed attempt to convince him to take the position offered him by the Los Angeles hospital, Georgia chose the safer topic of Ross's "adorable pooch." Beth was surprised, for she couldn't remember Georgia showing the slightest interest in any of the dogs, let alone Ross's mastiff.

"I had him less than a month before coming here," Ross told Georgia. "Saxon belonged to a friend from med school who had to give him up." He looked at Beth. "Can you imagine keeping a dog like that locked in a third-floor apartment all day and night?"

"It sounds like your friend had a mastiff for all the wrong reasons," Beth offered.

Matt roused from his reverie. "A dog like that would be the perfect icebreaker for meeting women."

Georgia gave Matt a playful poke in the ribs. "Men! Using the poor creature like that." She turned back to Ross. "How nice of you to take in Anglo."

"Saxon," Ross corrected. "But my circumstances for keeping a dog in the city were only slightly better than Bill's. Still, I thought that when I visited Rebecca, her love for the giant breeds might lead her to adopt Saxon."

Georgia was difficult for Ross to escape, but after lunch he managed to do so long enough to ask Beth to find out what was bothering Matt. "He puts me off with jokes," Ross told her. "Maybe you'll have better luck. We need to know if his current mood has to do with Rebecca or with something his mother is up to."

Beth caught up with Matt and Yvonne as they were about to enter their suite of rooms. "Arnie's off for a few days," she told Matt. "If you can spare the time, I'd appreciate a hand with the training this afternoon."

If Yvonne's eyes had been daggers, Beth's flesh would have fallen in ribbons to the floor. She could tell Yvonne was outraged to find "the hired help" making overtures to her son. He agreed to Beth's plan, and she was relieved to see that, unlike his mother, Matt didn't appear to think the dogs were an excuse for Beth to flirt with him.

Beth and Matt stepped outside into a strong prelude to the winds Louisa had predicted. High overhead, treetops swayed and whispered among themselves. Clumps of rust-colored twigs were detaching themselves from their branches and beginning slow spirals to the earth.

"This is really early," Matt said. "Usually the big winds don't come for another month or two."

"It looks like it's snowing!" Beth cried. "Look! Copper-colored flakes falling as slowly as snow—and as silently. Some are big as saucers!"

"Watch out," Matt warned her. "Here comes a platter."

A foot-wide piece fell more swiftly to the ground.

Beth was incredulous. "This happens every year?"

Matt headed for the kennels. "We'd better know the path by heart. The duff will cover it in no time. Frank spends a lot of September raking it clear again."

Beth passed Matt when he stopped to look up at the slow-falling twigs. She stopped too.

"I'm glad I was here to see this again," he said in a sad voice. "During the summer some of the spring's new growth turns yellow, then this copper color. When the winds come, they clear away the dry stuff and leave the trees tidy and green for winter." He bit thoughtfully at his lip. "Wouldn't it be great to shed your mistakes and false starts like that? To free yourself up for a fresh future?"

Matt's usual devil-may-care look had slipped to reveal

surprisingly vulnerable features. "Would you like to forget about helping me out today?" Beth asked. "Did I catch you at a bad time?"

He looked away. "No, I'd rather be busy. I just turned down a job offer, and I'm having regrets. Let's go." He headed off again toward the kennels.

She caught him by the sleeve. "If you're having regrets, maybe you should accept the offer."

"Right!" he said briskly. "And live with my mother's constant reminders of how disappointed she is in me?"

"If you'd be happy at this job, why should she be anything but happy for you?"

Matt shook his head. "You don't know my mother. She couldn't face her bridge club if her son dropped out of college to become a minor administrator and golf instructor at a small country club. She's threatened to pull up stakes and move from Sacramento if I 'disgrace' her like that. I don't want her misery on my conscience."

"You're good at golf?"

"Darn good! It's the only thing I've ever excelled at— and I love the game. I could have gone pro, or at least made a run for it. But that takes years of someone bankrolling you until you break into the prize money. I'm not saying I'm the best there is, but I know I could have garnered enough attention to land a spot as a club pro."

"Your mother wouldn't help you out?" Beth asked softly.

Matt's laugh was bitter. "Oh, she helped me compete in countless genteel tournaments—amateur, of course— where I might make the 'right connections' with the business tycoons who were eager, or so she believed, to offer me positions in their firms. Golf was okay as a hobby, but as far as her helping me develop it as a *career*—forget it!''

''And Rebecca?''

Matt shook his head firmly. ''I couldn't ask her. She would have agreed only as a means of lording it over my mother. I wasn't about to get into the middle of a tug-of-war that could only end up hurting Mom.''

Beth brought them both to a halt. ''The job offer, is it still open?''

''Not for long. An old buddy of mine runs this golf club, and he thinks the job's made for me. He needs to fill the slot soon. Georgie thinks I should take it.''

Beth couldn't remember feeling more warmly about Georgia. ''Your cousin's right. She's thinking of your happiness. You can tell me it's none of my business, but if I were your cousin—'' She broke off to swallow the lump tightening round her throat. ''If I were your cousin, I'd lead you straight back to the phone and dial your friend's number for you.''

''Really?''

She met his doubtful gaze. ''Really.''

''Well,'' Matt said thoughtfully, ''I guess I could ask him for a couple of days to think it over.''

She gave him a little push toward the house. ''I'd better work the dogs without you. There's no telling how a golf pro's touch might throw them off!''

Beth was afraid Ross and Aunt Jen would think that by cutting short her session with Matt she botched the chance to draw him out so she could check his alibi for the day Rebecca broke her hip. Aunt Jen, however, put that matter to rest when Beth returned to the house.

Beth thought she had been transported to the wildest edge of the world until she looked around her. The pickup had pulled into a small parking lot. At the opposite end of the lot, a neat cinder-block rest room facility stood behind a sign that proclaimed the site, Lost Whale Cove, to be a county park. Its door missing, a single telephone booth braved the elements and promised that civilization was only a coin away.

Matt helped Beth out of the pickup. "We'll have to let Georgia think she's the first to know," he said in a low voice, "but before I say anything to her—"

"Your friend is holding the position open!" Beth quickly whispered.

"Better than that. I went ahead and accepted it. And I just wanted to thank you for setting me in motion." With that, he pulled her into a friendly hug.

Though they drew apart almost at once, it was not soon enough. Ross and Georgia stood staring at them. Georgia broke into an impish smile and wagged a finger at Matt. Ross looked so startled that for a fleeting moment Beth felt as though she owed him an explanation. Then he headed straight for the telephone booth. He returned almost immediately, explaining he had had no luck checking on Rebecca's progress.

His manner was now so calm and relaxed that Beth decided she had mistaken his reaction moments before. *Business as usual,* she thought, trying to rally herself with the bargain she had made with Ross and Aunt Jen. This time, however, the phrase felt hollow. Her heart wasn't in it. Her heart, she was chagrined to discover, was elsewhere, drifting down a path it received no encouragement to explore.

Matt broke the silence. "I have something to tell you, Georgie," he began. "Just remember that I'm counting on you to stand by me when the gnashing of teeth begins." He paused to exaggerate a deep breath. "I'll need you there now that I'm definitely going the 'golf bum' route."

Georgia flew to Matt and drew him into a childlike circle of joyous hops and skips. "A golf *expert*, you mean!"

Beth slipped to the side of the truck and covered Irma's hamper with straw. Ross joined her.

"What's that all about?" he asked.

"For Arnie," she said. "He's supposed to look us up at sunset. I'll slip away and tell him where this is."

"What was *that* all about," Ross repeated, motioning toward the two cousins still congratulating each other.

"Oh, it's about a career move for Matt."

"It's *all* been about a career move for Matt?" Ross was smiling, but his gaze was searching. "All of it?"

Beth met that gaze and realized what it was asking. Until that instant she had never understood what was meant by "electricity" passing between two people. But this spark arcing from Ross's eyes to hers clearly had nothing to do with watts or amps. Their hands were inches from completing the circuit when Georgia bounded up. Beth couldn't answer Ross's question with Georgia there. She turned to the task of lifting the beach towels and blankets out of the truck.

"Ross and I will haul those," Georgia said, drawing off one blanket as her share. "You and Matt can bring the ice chest. You have the right shoes for it."

Beth saw what Georgia meant as the four of them made

their way down the battered and sun-bleached stairs leading halfway to the cove. After the stairs ended, the trail
cut steeply through rock and sand. Georgia's sandals were
definitely wrong for the uneven path. To steady herself
she leaned on Ross's arm. At one point Georgia lost her
footing. When Ross bent to right her, an electronic paging
device slipped from his jacket pocket.

"You didn't bring *that!*" Georgia protested.

Ross retrieved the pager. "Guilty."

"Luckily," Georgia said, "it won't work this far out."

"True," Ross said, "but I can use the phone where
we parked to check on Rebecca."

By the time they set up a picnic site to Georgia's
specifications, sunset was only an hour away. The clouds
hovering over the ocean's western horizon promised a
spectacular display of color. Beth couldn't imagine a
more romantic setting. But she had no trouble picturing
a more romantic *situation*, one with far less wind—and
absolutely none of this monopolizing of Ross by Georgia.

All at once the mastiff stood and faced the dense stand
of saplings on high ground near the far end of the cove.
Then he loped off in that direction. When Saxon failed
to respond to Ross's call or her own, Beth rose.

"I'll handle it," she said, hoping Ross realized that
Saxon's behavior could mean he spotted Arnie or Lurgan.

She reached for the dog whistle in her pocket but realized it could bring Lurgan as well as Saxon. It wasn't
the kind of whistle a human could hear, so Arnie wouldn't
have any warning to stop Lurgan before the wolfhound
responded. Beth didn't want Matt or Georgia to see Lurgan. They might let the information slip in front of
Louisa.

Saxon vanished into the stand of trees. To Beth's dismay Matt caught up with her when she was halfway there.

"I didn't want to be a third wheel," he said.

Beth tried to sound stern. "Well, take a hike for now. This is a training matter—I'll join you when I have Saxon."

Matt seemed surprised by her tone. Before he could recover, however, she had left him behind.

From the spot where Saxon had disappeared, a small creek led to the sea. The stream meandered over rocks, then flattened out once it reached the tidal sands. Beth guessed that Saxon splashed up the creek and disappeared into the stand of alders. To keep her feet dry, she made her way through the dense saplings, bending them from her path.

Ahead in the creek stood Arnie, wearing high rubber boots and waiting with both dogs. He explained he was camped just upstream next to a spring that fed the creek. "A couple of old guys are camped there too," he told Beth.

Beth could see that he was eager to share his exploits, but she was afraid Matt might catch up with her again. She told Arnie where to find the hamper and warned him to stay out of sight. "You're doing a great job," she added.

She returned through the saplings with Saxon tied to the neck cord of the dog whistle. Once they were in the open again, she removed the makeshift leash and kept a firm grip on Saxon's collar so he wouldn't rejoin Lurgan.

Matt was idling near the creek. "Let's take the long way back," he said. "Georgie needs time alone with Ross."

Beth didn't like what Matt was saying or the way he studied her expression when he said it.

He began chuckling. "That's the best way for Georgie to see that things won't work out. Anyone but my stubborn cousin can see that Ross's interests lie elsewhere."

Beth thought of the look that had passed between Ross and her earlier. She felt her cheeks flame to life.

Matt laughed heartily this time. "So I'm right. But how have you two workaholics found a moment to express any interest in each other?"

In all honesty Beth could counter with, "Don't be silly—the subject's never come up."

Matt laughed again. "I'm sorry for Georgie, of course, but it's just a matter of time before she realizes Ross isn't the man she wants to fall in love with. He isn't interested in the country-club life Georgie craves. Once she realizes that, she'll see that she's fallen for a fantasy instead of the man in front of her."

Beth threw him a thoughtful glance. "At heart you're really sensitive—"

"For a golf bum?" Matt interjected.

"Give yourself more credit," Beth scolded gently. "The way you feel about your cousin—even about the redwoods—shows you're more sensitive than you let people believe."

Matt shrugged. "All I'm doing is helping Georgia face a showdown between reality and her unrealistic dreams." He checked his watch. "Speaking of showdowns, the second generation should be gearing up for theirs right now."

"Second generation?"

"Georgie's folks and my mother. I've never seen Mom as nervous as she is about tonight."

"You've lost me," Beth admitted.

Matt grimaced. "Surely you caught wind of the summit conference scheduled for tonight? History's in the making about now—family history. Mom, Louisa, and Paul are meeting to take a united stand on Rebecca and the estate."

"I thought your mother and Louisa weren't speaking!"

"They're not. But if anything can unite them temporarily, it's the way Rebecca has been acting the past year—*impossible*. Beginning the cease-fire negotiations won't be easy, though. I guess Paul intends to serve as interpreter. This is all his idea. He's arranged everything—dinner in a private dining room where they can hash things out without making a spectacle of themselves."

Matt pointed to the picnic site. Ross was heading back up the path to his pickup. "Poor Georgie," he muttered.

Since their reason for staying away had ended, Beth and Matt rejoined Georgia, who looked thoughtful and subdued. She brushed sand from her ankles. "Ross wanted to call the hospital to check on Rebecca," she told them. She shivered.

The breeze had picked up. Matt wrapped a blanket around Georgia's shoulders before wandering down the beach.

The sun hovered over the distant clouds rimming the horizon. Soon it would sink into them. Saxon was following Ross's progress up the hill and clearly wanted to join him. Glad to see he had forgotten about Lurgan, Beth loosed her hold on the mastiff's collar and sent him on his way.

She eyed Georgia, wondering if Ross had asked her about Rebecca's first fall. She decided to do so herself.

"Rebecca's lucky she didn't rebreak that hip. Your mother said you saw your grandmother's first accident. That must have been horrible for you."

Georgia jerked to attention. "It was! But I didn't see the actual fall. Just coming in to find her was bad enough. I ran into the hall to see what all the thumping was and saw the dog coming down the stairs. At first I didn't notice Rebecca stretched out at my feet. She just lay there—like she was dead! I didn't know what to do."

Beth tried to sound casual. "At your feet?"

Georgia's interest waned. She nodded vaguely and looked over to where Matt bent over something in the sand.

Beth realized that to hold Georgia's attention she had to place her in the center of the conversation. "How terrible for you! Alone with her at such a horrible time!"

Georgia roused from her reverie. "It was dreadful."

"Did you scream for help? Who heard you?"

"My father. Daddy ran down the stairs and lifted Rebecca's head to see if she was still breathing. I think I would have fainted if he hadn't been there."

Matt returned and handed Georgia a mussel shell the ocean had smoothed to a clear, midnight blue. "A pearl for the princess," he said.

Georgia sighed gloomily. "You *always* say that, but there's never a pearl."

A car's honk barely reached them through the noise of the surf and breeze. Beth and Matt looked up to see Ross with one arm stretched inside the open window of the pickup and the other one waving at them.

"I'll see what he wants," Beth said.

Georgia didn't seem to notice, but Matt did. His eyebrows flicked up and down over the amused and knowing look he threw Beth.

Beth's mind was racing. In no time she had scrambled up the sand and rock path and was onto the rickety stairs. Keeping time with each step she took, Georgia's words thundered through her brain: *"I saw the dog coming down the stairs, but at first I didn't notice Rebecca stretched out at my feet. . . . Daddy ran down the stairs and lifted Rebecca's head to see if she was still breathing."*

Ross was back at the telephone when Beth reached him. By then she was certain of one thing—both Georgia and Paul claimed they had been on the ground floor when Rebecca fell.

One of them is mistaken—or lying. Out of breath, she tried to gasp this out to Ross.

He cut her off. "I've got to get to the hospital. Apparently Rebecca got a disturbing phone call and is insisting on checking herself out without a doctor's permission. They'll try to stall her until I can get there and talk some sense into her."

Beth fought for breath. "I just learned . . . Georgia and Paul . . . their stories . . . contradict each other."

Ross frowned. "Then maybe I'd ought to go straight home. What if Rebecca bosses her way out of the hospital before I get there? We don't want her facing Paul—or Louisa and Yvonne—without either of us there."

"They've all gone out . . . for dinner."

Ross looked relieved. "That's right. Gram said something like that was brewing. If they aren't home, then I guess it's safe for me to try to head off Rebecca at the hospital. I just found out that our suspicions of foul play are well founded. Rebecca's blood tests are back, and they prove she ingested far more of her sedative than even an accidental doubling of her medication could account for.''

Beth's eyes grew round. ''Then someone drugged her and slipped onto the deck once she was asleep! They doctored the dog leash to blame Lurgan, released the brake on the wheelchair—then pushed it!''

Ross caught Beth by the shoulders. ''I've got to hurry. Can you stay and phone the Smythes? Warn them that Rebecca might be on her way home. If she does show up, tell them not to leave her alone until we're back. I dialed the house while I waited for you, but the line was busy.''

''Okay. But what if I can't get through, either?''

''Call the sheriff's office and ask for Nick Lemley. Ask him to get right over to the house and follow up on what he and I talked about yesterday. I'm sorry to leave you stranded—yet it's just as well that Georgia and Matt will be stranded here too. That's exactly how we want them until we're sure who's at the bottom of things.''

''It isn't Matt!'' Beth cried. ''He wasn't around when Rebecca fell down the stairs! But this is no time to argue if you're going to catch Rebecca. Is there anything else?''

''Just this.'' Without warning, Ross kissed her.

It was a tentative kiss, but to Beth it was everything. It was a question, searching for her answer. It was a promise. And then he was gone.

The sky was now an inverted bowl of orange and fiery pink that spilled across the ocean from the western horizon. Beth felt as though the glow were setting her heart on fire. Before she realized it, the pickup was pulling away with Ross in it. She could only return his wave.

She ordered herself to get to work. Ross had put a leash on Saxon and tied him to a nearby bench. He also had left a pile of coins by the telephone. Beth let one dime chase the other down the pay phone before she dialed the Malvern number. The line was no longer busy, but the connection was so frayed with static that Beth could barely make out Aunt Jen's voice quaver, "Hello."

"I'm so glad it's you!" Aunt Jen cried once Beth identified herself. "Ross has to get to the hospital—"

"We know," Beth interrupted. "To stop Rebecca."

Saxon let out a happy bark. Beth caught sight of Arnie and Lurgan at the far edge of the parking area.

"He's too late," Aunt Jen said. "A taxi company called to say that Rebecca was on her way home and wanted all of us to keep away from her dogs or else. But never mind that! Ross must get to the hospital for Arnie's sake. Irma just heard Arnie was in a car accident. She and Frank have left for the hospital and want Ross to meet them there."

Beth's heart stopped. "Something's wrong, Aunt Jen. I'm looking at Arnie this minute. He's perfectly fine."

"Oh, thank heavens!" Aunt Jen cried.

Beth's hand shook. "Aunt Jen, do you realize what this means? Either a horrible trick has been played on the Smythes—or someone wants them out of the house!"

Crackling across the wires punctuated Aunt Jen's voice. "But who would do such a thing?"

Beth held her breath. "Did Yvonne and the Carstairs's go out to dinner as planned?"

"My, yes. They drove away over an hour ago."

"That buys us some time," Beth said. "It's a long way into town and back."

"Oh, but they've only gone to—" Static erupted on the line, making Aunt Jen's next word sound like "Holland."

Beth had a crazy image of Yvonne, Paul, and Louisa disembarking from a jet and heading past windmills to visit a tulip farm. "Where?" she shouted. "How far away is it?"

"Speak up, dear," Aunt Jen said. "The wind's playing havoc with the wires. Branches are falling left and right. We lost the electricity an hour ago and are lucky the phone lines are still standing."

Beth spoke as loudly and distinctly as she could. "Aunt Jen, this is important! When Rebecca shows up, get in the taxi and head straight back to the hospital!"

"You'll have to speak up, dear. Oh! Someone's here."

"Hurry!" Beth shouted. "If it's the taxi, get in it and leave immediately. If it's not the taxi—then *hide* yourself until Ross or I get there!"

"Beth! Whatever's the matter?"

"There's no time to explain," Beth began.

As if to confirm her words, the line went dead.

Beth stared at the silent receiver. Then she collected herself and motioned frantically for Arnie to join her. She hadn't caught all of what Aunt Jen said about Yvonne, Paul, and Louisa's plans for the evening—but she didn't like the sound of the word "only." "They *only* went to—" Aunt Jen had said. "Only" meaning they *only* went to a mediocre restaurant? Or "only" as in *only* down the road, not far away?

She found the sheriff's number in a phone book puffed like a marshmallow from its exposure to the elements. She dialed and was relieved to hear that her end of the line was working. When they couldn't connect her with Ross's contact, Nick Lemley, the best Beth could do was to pass along Ross's message and stress its urgency. By the time she hung up, Arnie had joined her.

He was looking all around. "Where's Mom's hamper?"

"You won't be needing it. We have to hurry back to the house. But first, is there someplace around here—a town or even just a spot on the map—called 'Holland'?"

Arnie shook his head

Beth tried again. "Somewhere people go all dressed up for dinner?"

Arnie bit his lip. "You mean *Hollands'*? The Hollands run a bed-and-breakfast place. They're supposed to serve real fancy food. I don't know if people who aren't staying there can come to—"

"Where is it?" Beth interrupted. "How far is it from your home?"

Arnie looked perplexed. "Well, it's a long drive. They live clear over on High Ridge Road."

Beth relaxed slightly. "That buys us a little time."

"But it's a lot faster," Arnie continued, "just to walk there through the woods."

Understanding hit Beth as swiftly as a last ray from the dying sun now pierced the cloud bank. For one instant sunlight gilded Arnie, Lurgan, and everything else in Beth's sight. Then all faded into gloom. Because there was no time to think, Beth felt rather than thought what would happen if she didn't get back to the house in time.

"Take me to your dad's truck," she said. "This is an emergency, Arnie. Run! I'll follow."

She paused long enough to untie Saxon. Before she

could remove the leash from his collar, he bounded off after Lurgan and Arnie. She hurried to catch up with them. They ran a quarter of a mile through the dusk. Luck was with the mastiff; his leash did not catch on the brush.

This time the course was chiefly downhill, so Beth had enough breath left when they reached the campsite to tell Arnie about the phone call that had sent his parents hurrying to the Eureka hospital. She was hoping Arnie would go with her to the Malvern estate but understood at once why he was far more concerned about his parents and what they must be feeling than he was about what she quickly sketched out about Rebecca's situation. *Besides,* she told herself, *it isn't fair to drag him into danger.*

Two older campers who had eavesdropped on Beth and Arnie's hurried exchange now offered to take Arnie to the hospital to meet his parents and clear things up.

"You're too worried to drive, son," one said, clapping Arnie on the shoulder.

Arnie turned over the keys to his father's truck to Beth.

"What about the dogs?" the remaining camper asked her. "They're too big to ride in Turner's car, but we can't just leave them here. No telling when any of us will get back."

"They'll have to come with me," Beth said impatiently, scrambling into the cab of the pickup. With a sinking heart she noticed the stick shift, something she hadn't wrestled with for years. "I need a refresher course!" she cried.

The older of the two campers came to her aid and ran her through the "H" of shifting gears. To her dismay, Beth noticed that the other camper had climbed into the back of the pickup and was tying Saxon there.

"There's no time for that!" Beth shouted.

"It's the law!" the man snapped. When she started the engine, however, he quickly got off the truck.

Beth pulled away. Everything was fine until she left the campground's uneven road and had to shift gears to speed up. The pickup lurched forward. In the rearview mirror she saw the dogs thrown against each other. They staggered to keep their footing. Saxon was securely tied, but now she could see that Lurgan wasn't. *There's no time to stop,* she told herself, driving on.

Her parents had always praised her for having a good sense of direction. For the first time in her life, Beth prayed they were right. She hadn't paid close attention to the route Ross had driven to the beach. That ride hadn't taken long, but now every curve picked out by the headlights seemed hours in coming.

Suddenly she remembered Ross's electronic pager and chided herself for not thinking to call the hospital and ask them to page him with the emergency message that he was needed immediately back at home. But doing so would have cost precious moments, moments that might make all the difference in saving her grandmother's life.

When Arnie told her the Hollands' place was close by the Malvern house, Beth had *seen*—in a swift succession of vivid images—what would happen if she didn't make it back in time. Those images had flown past in silence because there had been no time then for words. Now, however, the missing words caught up with Beth. The first ones echoing through her mind were from something she had heard so often in recent days, she knew it by heart:

"Sometimes I'll be sitting in a restaurant and the pain

becomes so killing, I simply must get out to walk, walk, walk it off."

Paul Carstairs setting up his perfect alibi.

Beth thought of the emphasis he always seemed to put on "killing." She sped up. She pictured Paul sitting, at that very moment, at an elegantly appointed table, readying himself to leave the two half-sisters to glare each other down. He would rise, feigning pain, and excuse himself to walk, walk, walk through the woods, woods, woods—back home.

He counted on Rebecca being there—and now she would be, thanks to that "disturbing phone call" Ross mentioned. Without Lurgan to blame for another "accident," what did Paul have in mind this time?

Beth felt the blood drain from her fingers gripping the steering wheel. It must have been Paul who saw to it that the Smythes would be gone, leaving only Aunt Jen at home. Was she included in his deadly plans for his mother-in-law?

For the next few miles she felt too numb to think. All she could manage to do was steer the big truck she wasn't used to through the darkening forest. She swung wide around a blind curve, thankful she had met no traffic for miles. When a car finally did come from the opposite direction, Beth was dismayed to discover that it was a taxi. Except for its driver, it was empty.

Rebecca's home! Aunt Jen didn't make it out with her!

The road now led due east through dense trees. Ahead, a distant hill wore a halo, courtesy of a moon ready to rise. Beth sensed rather than saw the turnoff to the Malvern estate. She half expected to find another sawhorse blocking her way and was prepared, this time, to drive right over or through it.

She wished she knew the driveway well enough to navigate it without the truck's telltale headlights, but she didn't want to drive as slowly as it would take to slip up unnoticed to the house. There was no time. She had to roar the truck in and take her chances on beating Paul home and driving Aunt Jen and Rebecca to safety. She didn't know what she would do if Paul was already there.

Beth braked hard at the foot of the front steps and left the engine running when she jumped out of the cab. She cleared the steps two at a time, then threw wide one section of the double doors. The electricity was out. Two kerosene lamps dimly lit the front hall. Running in, Beth nearly hurled herself into two frightened women.

Rebecca sat in her wheelchair, her face ashen in the flickering lantern light. For once the stern matriarch had nothing to say. Her strong hands lay limp and helpless in her lap.

"Thank goodness it's you!" Aunt Jen cried. "Rebecca's taxi was already here when the phone went out. No sooner had the driver helped her into the wheelchair than she shooed him off. I didn't make it downstairs in time to catch him." She held out something that jangled. "Yours were the only car keys I could scare up—we were just about to make a run for it."

"You're alone?" Beth gasped. At Aunt Jen's nod, Beth rushed on. "There's no time to lose. But we may need the gun."

"Rebecca went for it while I got these." Aunt Jen jangled the keys again. "But she said her gun was gone!"

"*This* gun, ladies?"

Beth wheeled to face the door. There stood Paul Carstairs, gun in hand.

If the situation hadn't been so grave, Beth might have laughed. The pockets of Paul's linen suit bulged like pack saddles. He had rolled his pant legs up to his knees, revealing thin ankles and calves wrapped in socks the same pale pink as his tie.

"Dear, dear, *Beth*," he said, "please come over here by me. I didn't expect to find you, and I need to make sure you aren't packing any nasty surprises." His smile was brittle. "Taken aback to discover that I know your true name? Don't be. Rebecca has no secrets from me."

Beth did as she was told.

Rebecca came to life and leaned forward in her wheelchair. "You've snooped in my mail for years. I always knew that!"

Paul cocked his head. "But you thought it would be different with the detective you hired last spring, didn't you? Having him send his reports addressed to Irma wasn't your cleverest idea, Mommy dearest. I asked myself why dull, plodding Irma Smythe would receive mail from the highest-priced detective agency in the state. Certainly that boring husband of hers wasn't up to any hanky-panky. Of course, I just *had* to investigate." As he spoke, he methodically patted each of Beth's pockets. "Empty that one," he told her.

Beth's eyes briefly met her grandmother's. *You knew. You knew who I was all along.* Then she reached into her pocket and drew forth her wallet and the dog whistle.

"I'd better have them both," Paul said. He pocketed the wallet but shook the whistle in Beth's face. "We can't have you using this if Louisa has been up to her old trick of letting the dogs out to police the grounds. My wife's diversions have been amusing, even unexpectedly helpful at times, but I want no additional surprises tonight.'' He turned back to Aunt Jen. ''I'd better have those too,'' he said, using the gun to point to the car keys she still held before her. ''Retrieve them, dear Beth, and hand them over.''

Again Beth did as told. For one moment she held in her hand Lewis Elliott's keys, warmed by Aunt Jen's touch. Her fingers closed round the keepsake Lewis kept on his key chain, a battered silver whistle, the first trophy he ever won for showing dogs. Then Paul took the keys, snatching away the slight comfort they had brought her.

He sighed. ''Aunt Jen, you know I always *tried* to like you. But you've disappointed me lately with your nosy phone calls about Yvonne and Matt's whereabouts the day Rebecca took her little tumble. Thus, I'm afraid you've brought this on yourself.'' He sighed again. ''Poor Ross. But then, his grief and resentment will find a deserving target once he learns of this young woman's duplicity in coming here under a false name. He'll concur with the authorities that Beth and her deranged sister are to blame.

''Dear, dear Beth!'' Paul continued. ''You think you've thrown me for a loop by popping up like this, don't you? But, no! I view it as a windfall. Now I can manage everything in one fell swoop. But first, we need to make these other ladies *secure,* if not comfortable. To Rebecca's den, all of you. Beth, bring a lamp to light our way. Stay directly in front of my 'helper.' '' On his last word, he waved the gun.

They all did as ordered. Light flickering from the lamp Beth held cast grotesque shadows along the walls. Once they were inside the den, Paul headed for the desk.

"My, but you're quiet tonight, Rebecca," he began. "Perhaps you'll want to comment on this?" He pulled forth a small key and opened the desk with it.

"You despicable worm!" Rebecca hissed.

Paul feigned surprise. "As I said, you have no secrets from me." He found and held aloft a thick manila file. "Here it is—the detective agency's report. Let's see, we'll need to put it over there." He moved to a heavy metal file box atop a bookcase.

Beth stared at the box. She used one just like it for important records at Barking Up the Wrong Tree. The box's only virtue was that it was fireproof. Beth drew a sharp breath, struck by what that implied. She grabbed the back of Rebecca's wheelchair to steady herself.

"Oh!" Paul exclaimed to himself. He was looking through the metal file box. "Here's that missing letter from Jenny Orne. We can't leave that lying around." He emptied one of his bulging pockets, piling a tangle of rope onto the desk. Then he pocketed the letter.

"My sister never wrote that!" Beth cried.

Paul put the file into the metal box and shut the fasteners. "But of course she did," he said evenly. "The detective's report all but confirms it. The technical terms didn't fool me. I read through the rigamarole and figured out—just as the authorities are sure to—that your sister's crazy. All those years of treatment and special doctors! The report says she has to be supervised constantly. So it stands to reason that she's grown sly and has figured out how to work around her keepers. By now she's found someone—perhaps a fellow patient, also crazy—to do her dirty work. Or at least that was my *old* plan."

Aunt Jen let out an indignant gasp.

Paul shook a finger at her. "Now, now. It's really quite plausible. You've seen the photos, Aunt Jen. Our poor, mad Jenny is quite a beauty. Lots of men, sane or crazy, might kill for her."

That single word, "kill," hung in the air like a knife. Beth had been ready to contradict him, to tell him Jenny was autistic, not crazy. But now she sensed that Paul's ignorance of Jenny's true situation might be the only thing to save Jenny from him. *If I'm gone.*

She caught in Aunt Jen's eye a look that seemed to echo that thought. The two of them joined hands.

"I'm glad to see you on such good terms," Paul said. "That should make this next part easier. Please take a seat in the desk chair, Aunt Jen." He picked up the tangle of rope and held it out to Beth. "You should find just enough to tie both ladies' wrists to the arms of their chairs. Make sure you do a proper job. I'll check your handiwork. If I'm not perfectly satisfied—well, let's just say that both ladies will be very, very sorry."

Beth could only obey. All she could hope for was that Paul would grow careless and leave her an opening. What she would try to do, she wasn't sure—but she was determined to seize whatever opportunity came her way.

He bowed slightly toward Rebecca. "Good night, ladies! I'm afraid we have to run. Beth, bring the light."

Beth had time to exchange one last look with Aunt Jen. *I'll think of something,* she hoped her eyes promised. Holding on to that promise—even if it proved empty— was better for Aunt Jen and Rebecca than waiting helplessly in the dark for Paul's sinister plan to take effect.

Rebecca flared to life as Paul closed the door. Her curses followed Paul and Beth halfway to the basement.

Beth had never been down there before. Vast and dark, the basement smelled of damp cement and contained little more than a huge furnace at one end and a washer and dryer at the other.

"Gather up the laundry from the chute and pile it on those empty boxes I so conveniently left nearby." As he spoke, Paul pulled a flashlight from his pocket and flicked it on.

When Beth finished, she automatically reached down to retrieve the kerosene lamp she had set at her feet.

"Leave it," he said, "and come with me." He led her to the furnace at the far end of the basement. He kept the gun on her as he toyed with a valve on a thin pipe. Then he opened a panel and looked inside the furnace. "Good," he murmured to himself. "Pilot light's off." He glanced at Beth. "Don't mind my chatter. It's just my endearing way of dealing with your unexpected appearance. Talking myself through each step will help me catch all the adjustments I'll need to make to the plan."

He reached for the nearby thermostat. "Lucky for us, this is the old-fashioned kind that isn't run by an electric switch. Now *that* would have been inconvenient! No telling when the power will come back on. There—that should release the propane slowly enough to give us a healthy head start. You can return to the lamp now, my dear."

Paul ordered Beth to remove the lamp's glass chimney and blow out the flame. "Unscrew the wick apparatus. Good. Now pour the kerosene over the laundry and boxes. Sprinkle it evenly—don't drain it all in one spot."

Beth noticed that his flashlight's beam was too narrow to follow all the fuel she scattered. She tossed it more wildly, hoping he wouldn't notice how much she wasted on the cold cement of the floor and wall. Maybe that would save the elderly sisters.

When she was finished, Beth turned to find Paul holding the flashlight and the gun together in one hand. She could see that any unexpected movement from her was now even more likely to set off his trigger finger. She held still and watched him pull from his pocket a piece of paper and something else she couldn't distinguish.

He held the paper in his teeth and spoke his next words through them. "Yes, Jenny Orne's last letter—and certainly my crowning achievement. However, I can't have anyone in law enforcement admiring it too closely." A small flame erupted from his free hand. He held it toward Beth.

She accepted what she now made out to be a cigarette lighter that Paul had ignited with one hand.

Next he retrieved the paper from his teeth, wadded it, and held it out to Beth. "I'll let you do the honors. Light it, stand back, then throw it onto the pile. Then I want you starting up the stairs right in front of me. If my 'helper' loses contact with your spine before we're out of the house, you'll spoil everything and make both of us very sorry."

Beth's mind raced. *He isn't planning to kill me in the house. Once we're out in the dark, maybe I can get away.*

She did as directed, relieved to see how small the first flames were. Halfway up the stairs, however, Beth heard the roar of the pile really catching fire. She could only pray it would go out before the room filled with gas.

"I just realized why you dropped into my lap!" Paul cried suddenly. "You've been talking to Georgia, haven't you? I *knew* that her unscheduled homecoming might gum up the works. It was just a matter of time before someone poked around the discrepancies between our versions of Rebecca's tumble down the stairs. Never mind. After tonight no one will think to rehash that old business. I'll leave them plenty of new material to puzzle over.''

They hurried through the house and stepped out onto the porch. The winds had temporarily died down. The moon had risen enough to illuminate the two dogs in the back of the truck. They looked expectantly in Beth's direction. The engine still idled, just as Beth had left it.

"We can't have *that*," Paul said. "That looks too spontaneous. It must appear as though you came armed with a well-calculated plan. Turn off the ignition."

He kept the gun at her back as they walked down the steps. Once the truck was silent, he shone the flashlight onto the dogs. Saxon leaned over the truck's side, his taut leash caught in the light.

"Good," Paul murmured to himself. "They're tied up."

Beth's mind snagged on his words. *But Lurgan isn't tied.* It was a small mistake for Paul to make, but it was the first she had caught. It gave her hope that he might make another.

Paul shone the flashlight onto his watch. "With all your help, dear Beth, we're running a bit ahead of schedule. In case I ever needed a plan such as tonight's, I conditioned everyone to expect my sciatica-relief walks to take up to an hour—but the shorter I'm gone, the better." He turned the light onto her.

Beth quickly closed her eyes.

"Let's see," he mused. "Your arrival means I have

to retrieve something I didn't think I'd need until tomorrow, when I intended to deal with you. It's in the
garage—and that gives me an idea! As long as we're
going where the cars are, you might as well drive me
partway back. That will save even more time."

In the garage Paul set the flashlight so that it lit up an
old harrow and freed his hand. He reached gingerly behind the old farm machine and pulled out a flat, plastic
bag. As careful as he was trying to be, he nonetheless
rose with a dark smudge on his pants. "Well, it could
have been worse," he mumbled, shrugging.

Beth saw what he meant. Once his pant leg was un-
rolled, the smudge wouldn't show. Now it was clear why
the impeccable Paul Carstairs had allowed himself to look
so ridiculous that night. He didn't want his cuffs betraying
either his journey through the woods or any telltale
smudges from his deadly task.

From the plastic bag he first removed a paper towel,
then used that to carefully pull out what looked like a
half sheet of paper. He worked slowly, careful to keep
the gun trained on Beth even when, as in the basement,
his gun hand was needed to perform an additional task.

She understood at once the purpose of the paper towel.
So he won't leave fingerprints. She was chilled by how
carefully he had plotted out the smallest details. Would
it be possible to trip up such a calculating mind? She had
caught him overlooking only one thing, and that scarcely
mattered. Because he himself was so methodical, Paul
had assumed that one dog tied to the truck meant the
other dog must be tied too.

A seed of hope sent out a taproot into the darkness that
trapped Beth. *He said I would drive him partway back.*

She had the beginning of a plan, a plan given her, in part, by Paul himself, back in the front hall. But to surprise a man who worked out so many possibilities ahead of time and left nothing to chance, Beth knew that she, too, must leave nothing to chance.

She raised her empty hands to her face, cupped them, and blew breath hoarsely into them.

The flashlight beam nailed her. "What are you up to?" Paul demanded.

"I'm cold," she said in a small voice. She blew again into her hands, then rubbed them vigorously.

He seemed to lose interest. Outside, the wind picked up, battered the garage door a few seconds, then died.

Paul dropped the plastic sack into a waste barrel. Clearly his fingerprints on that didn't matter. A member of the household, he was likely to clean out his car and toss out any garbage in the garage.

"Take this," he said, giving her the half sheet of paper but retaining the paper towel. He used it to open the passenger door of Lewis's car. "Get in."

He kept the gun leveled at her while she got behind the wheel. The car's interior light seemed garish after the gloom of the past half hour. Beth blinked at the paper Paul had given her. Then she realized what she was looking at. She held a half sheet bearing her own handwriting.

Lewis, she had written in huge letters, *forgive me!* In smaller letters she had signed, *Beth.*

She stared in disbelief, trying to recall writing the note. She almost recognized it, but something was wrong—something was missing. Then she remembered—this was only the top half of a note explaining to Lewis that she had mistakenly filled his tank with low-octane gas. That portion, she realized, must have been in a postscript now missing from the note.

Paul. Paul stole this from my room and cut half of it off. But why?

She became conscious of Paul sitting beside her, vigorously rubbing something with the paper towel. She saw that it was her wallet.

"Take it," he said, "and turn it over a few times."

My fingerprints! her mind screamed. *He needs some of my fingerprints back on it.* Once again the gun convinced her to do as he said.

"Now," he continued, "let's see what you have inside. Open it."

The wallet fell open to Beth's driver's license. It faced a faded family portrait from her childhood.

"The perfect touch!" Paul cried. "Take out the picture and fold it in that note you wrote."

Beth's fingers fumbled at the task. *More fingerprints,* she thought dully. When she finished, Paul ordered her to open the glove compartment and to place inside it the wallet and the note folded around the picture.

Now the full impact of what Paul had done to her message to Lewis struck Beth. *He's made it look like . . . like a suicide note!*

Chapter Ten

Beth struggled to keep herself from giving in to the numbing shock trying to embrace her now that she fully understood Paul's plans for her. *Keep your wits!* she tried to rally herself.

She pictured the systematic way her captor had set up his alibi. That reminded her to raise her hands, cup them, and vigorously blow into them. Any hope she had of living beyond the end of the drive might depend on conditioning Paul to ignore or at least take for granted that gesture.

Her heart sank when Paul put the keys into the ignition instead of handing them to her. She rolled down the window.

"I thought you were cold," he said testily.

"Yes, but I also feel dizzy," she explained. "I need fresh air, or I'll get sick to my stomach."

"No! Don't you dare do that!" he said, shuddering. "Drive," he added more forcefully.

Beth backed out of the garage and turned the car, as directed, down an extension of the driveway she had never driven. Through the open window they could smell something burning. Paul sniffed hard a few times and seemed satisfied with what he found.

"There," he said, keeping the gun on Beth as he

pointed with his free hand to what looked like a narrow clearing that disappeared into the dark forest. "It's an old logging road. Trust me—it's the way I came."

Beth turned off where he indicated. She glanced down at the odometer. She had to think of a way to keep from driving more than a quarter of a mile.

They slowly threaded their way through the trees until a huge and freshly fallen branch blocked their way.

"Get out and move it," Paul said. "Stay in the head-lights where I can see you."

Beth got out of the car and struggled through the springy layer of fresh duff. She realized she was strong enough to tug the enormous branch out of the way, but she pretended she couldn't do so. Between attempts, she paused to blow into her hands and rub them.

To calm her runaway heart, she tried to think of the headlights as the footlights Aunt Jen so thrived on when on stage. *I hope I inherited the acting gene she carries,* she thought, returning to the car. *Here goes.*

"I can't do it," Beth told him, trying to sound helpless as she sat wearily in the driver's seat. "It will take both of us to move it." Mentally she crossed her fingers, counting on the fastidious Paul Carstairs not to want to risk mussing his linen suit in a telltale way. To make sure he didn't miss that point, she added plaintively, "Look at all these snags!" She picked at nonexistent blemishes on her sleeves.

Her performance seemed to convince Paul. "Then this is as far as we go," he said, annoyed.

Beth turned off the ignition, pulling out the key. Quickly she turned off the headlights.

"Put those back on!" Paul snapped.

She complied, glad for the momentary distraction. She hoped it would make Paul forget about the keys. Taking care how she positioned them this time, she cupped her hands and raised them to her mouth. Then she blew hard into her hands, turning as much as she dared toward the door she had left partly open. The wind, she noticed, was nearly still.

Paul sighed wearily. "I had hoped for less of a walk, once I discovered I could have a chauffeur." He checked his watch.

Again Beth blew into her cupped hands, blew for all she was worth. This was her long shot. She also planned to make a break for it the first chance she got.

"Get out," Paul said, "This will have to do." Then he added more amiably. "I'll meet you in the headlights."

Beth blew into her hands once more before pretending to lumber wearily from the car. As soon as she was on her feet, she slammed the door.

She wheeled and ran back the way they had come. The duff was even harder to move through in the dark than it had been when she had help from the headlights. Either that—or Paul was too quick for her. Beth made it only twenty feet before his flashlight caught and betrayed her.

The gun exploded. For a split second Beth thought she had been shot, so violently did her body jerk in reaction to the sound. She froze before she realized she was fine— and should have kept running.

He had only fired a warning shot, she saw that now. *If his plan is to work, he needs to shoot me at close range.*

Paul closed in on her. "Over there," he said. "Don't get more than three feet ahead of me. Over there, in that open spot."

Beth looked ahead. A hundred feet ahead, the trees parted. A clear area lay bathed in moonlight. *Why does he want me so far from the car?*

Just then the wind picked up. More twigs spiraled to the earth. Beth's worst nightmares swam before her. She pictured herself, mortally wounded, fallen in the moonlit space ahead. There, she would slowly suffocate, buried by falling redwood branches and needles. She might not be found for days. As far as Paul was concerned, the longer, the better. The longer it took to find her, the colder his trail would grow.

Beth understood that once she stepped into that moonlight, there would be no way to hide. She needed a distraction. If only the cautious Paul would take a misstep in the tricky duff. Then she might escape the flashlight long enough to find a hiding place. Either that or her long shot would have to come through.

Once again Beth pretended to blow into her hands to warm them. With Paul to her back, she could afford to be less subtle about blowing into the battered dog whistle on Lewis's key chain. She had no idea whether the whistle even worked. For all she knew, Lewis retired it in the first place because it had ceased to function.

Thirty feet remained to the moonlit clearing. Thirty feet to sure death. Beth prayed for something—anything—to happen. *If only the wind would drop an enormous branch on Paul!*

But the redwoods had already shed most of their unwanted coats. Only a few dry twigs rained down on the path now. Then Beth thought she heard something. It was more crackling of branches, but what stirred her hope was the direction the sound came from—from ground level rather than from overhead. When the crackling stopped, Beth quickly put the old whistle to her lips and blew what she hoped were, for a dog, three ear-piercing calls.

"What are you up to now?" Paul growled. "Turn around! What do you have there? Give it to me!"

Beth blew again. Halfway through her second attempt, the gun slapped her across the face. The blow sent her reeling.

She spun around and caught a low branch. When it failed to steady her, she let go and clawed the air for balance. She heard Paul's gasp of surprise and realized the branch had slapped him. He dropped the flashlight.

Beth didn't hesitate. She ran, flinging herself wildly through the darkness. Half stunned by the blow, she realized too late that she had run straight for the moonlit clearing. She stopped on its fringe, but not in time to keep Paul from seeing her.

He fired another shot. It whizzed past her hip. This time, however, Beth knew better than to stop moving. Skirting the clearing's edge, she stayed just inside the darkness. She struggled ahead until she reached a huge tree. She dropped to her knees, scrambled to its far side, and stopped. She waited, hugging the enormous trunk, hoping against hope that Paul would run by.

At first all she could hear was her own heart, its thundering growing even louder once she made out the light moving closer. *Paul has the flashlight again and is coming after me!* The beam's erratic progress also told her that Paul must be hurrying to make up for lost time.

Then she heard something else. More branches crackling. A distinct padding. Now she was sure. *Lurgan!*

The wolfhound was coming—and true to his nature, he was chasing down whatever he heard running in the dark. She could hear Paul huffing hurriedly to her tree. Branches crackled all around him. Suddenly he shrieked in shock and disbelief.

The next instant something flew through the darkness and thumped down a few feet from Beth, crackling twigs as it went. She couldn't see what had fallen—which meant it wasn't the flashlight. Paul was carrying only one other thing. *The gun!*

She dove for it, expecting Paul to do the same. If she froze, leaving him to find it, he would stumble across her hiding spot in the bargain.

But Paul didn't come. "Help me!" he shrieked. His next words were strangely muffled.

Beth's fingers closed around the gun still clammy from Paul's grasp. She quickly made her way to the flashlight, now reduced to a copper glow in a drift of redwood duff. When she picked up the light and turned it on Paul, she was nearly as surprised as he must have been.

She expected to find Lurgan. And there he was, his huge tongue lolling in and out of his mouth, his breath blossoming like ghostly peonies in the cold air. But the huge mass pinning Paul to the ground was the same one that had greeted Beth in exactly this way the night of her arrival.

Saxon lay regally on Paul's chest, one enormous paw all but covering the man's face. From the mastiff's collar hung eighteen inches of leash, frayed at the end.

"Saxon!" Beth cried. "You chewed through your leash! You undisciplined, untrained, bad—*wonderfully* bad—dog!"

Thoughts of Aunt Jen and Rebecca cut through Beth's relief. She pulled Saxon off Paul and ordered him to turn facedown. When he didn't immediately respond, she released Saxon and found Paul easier to persuade the second time.

Next she fell back on years of helping vets restrain injured and frenzied animals. She undid Paul's tie and bound his hands securely behind his back in a fraction of the time it took to tie a four-legged creature. As for his legs, she decided all she needed to do was to tie his sturdy shoestrings tightly together.

A few more twigs fell as she worked.

"They'll cover me!" Paul whined. "You'll never find your way back here! I'll die before anyone can find me."

Beth suppressed the urge to remind him of what he had planned for her. "Don't worry," she said. "We can always send out the dogs."

When she had Paul trussed like a Thanksgiving turkey, Beth was up and moving fast, the dogs leading her home. *Home!* she thought, fighting the knot tightening round her throat. *Is it still standing? Are Aunt Jen and Rebecca still alive?*

She jogged too fast to get much use from Paul's flashlight. From time to time she nearly lost her footing, but now she considered the darkness before her a good omen. No blazing structure lit the sky. Maybe she would get there in time.

She slowed down when the house came into view. The electricity was still out, but several vehicles were parked in front, two with their headlights on bright. A flashing amber light topped one. Only then did Beth remember her hasty phone call to the sheriff's office with Ross's message. She was startled by the hue and cry that ensued when she came into view with the dogs.

"We've found her!" a man boomed. He ran up to Beth.

"The fire!" she cried. "Was anyone hurt?"

"Nope. It burned out before we got here. Good thing one of the residents thought to turn off the outside main to the propane tank when the electricity went off."

"That was me!" Aunt Jen's voice floated out from the nearest vehicle.

Beth shook off the man trying to give her a hand. She ran to the van she now recognized as the emergency vehicle that had carried off Rebecca only yesterday. She clambered inside and dimly made out two makeshift pallets.

"Aunt Jen!" she cried.

"I'm fine, dear," said the dark mass to her left. "I'm only going along to keep my sister company. See, Rebecca—I told you your granddaughter would keep her head and come out of this!"

No word came from the other side.

The man caught up to the van. "I need to strap you in, miss. You're all going to the hospital for a checkup. Doctor's orders."

Beth's heart rose. "Doctor? Ross?"

"Oh, dear," Aunt Jen said. "He's out in the party searching for you! Rebecca was able to crane her neck and watch through the window to see which way your car's taillights vanished. So two of the deputies went up the old logging road after Paul and you. Ross insisted on going with them. He'll be so relieved to find you here!"

The man shook his head. "We can't wait for them to

return.'' He pointed to the silent side of the emergency vehicle. ''That one may be going into shock.''

''I am not going into shock,'' Rebecca said. But her voice carried none of its usual venom or conviction.

Beth let herself be strapped in. A deputy sheriff rode along to take her statement. As they drove off, Beth caught sight of the three Smythes and knew the dogs would be taken care of. She wondered about Georgia and Matt but quickly realized that being stranded at a beach only minutes from a public telephone would be the least of the misfortunes Georgia would suffer this night.

''Poor Georgia,'' she murmured. She was glad Matt would be there to comfort his cousin when she heard the news about what her father had attempted to do.

The deputy sheriff finished questioning Beth and radioed back the essential details she gave him on where to look for Paul. Farther up the highway their vehicle paused to rendezvous with one driven by still another law officer on her way to the Malvern place. She took the deputy back with her.

Once the deputy was gone, Aunt Jen filled Beth in on several missing pieces of the puzzle. It turned out that both the Smythes and Rebecca had received calls from a man with an odd voice. In each case, the caller claimed to be an innocent bystander who had been stopped by an unidentified ''hysterical woman'' who asked him to make the phone call for her. Rebecca and the Smythes were so distracted by the alarming and urgent nature of the messages that they didn't think to question the caller, who clearly had been Paul disguising his voice.

The Smythes were told that the woman said she had just seen their son pulled from a terrible automobile wreck and taken by ambulance to the hospital. Next, Rebecca was called. She was told that the "hysterical woman" wouldn't talk directly to her because she didn't want to be identified and possibly lose her job. Supposedly the woman was an animal lover who had just overheard a vet agree to destroy all the Malvern dogs. She claimed the vet was already headed for the estate. When pressed for more information, the caller said he knew nothing other than what the woman had told him and he was just trying to do a good turn.

Beth shuddered. Once again, how clever Paul had been. He had known his victims well enough to gauge their reactions correctly. If the rest of his plan had worked as well, she had little doubt whom the authorities would be searching for by now. Not the "nice guy" who phoned just trying to help out. No, they'd be hunting for the "hysterical woman" who supposedly tricked him. She herself would have ended up as the chief suspect for that role.

The rest of the ride was a blur. Beth guessed that Aunt Jen talked more to keep up her sister's spirits than to pass on information. The only time Rebecca spoke was to respond when her sister chided her.

"This is ridiculous," Aunt Jen had said. "The county is only supposed to have this vehicle for demonstration purposes. Here you've gone and taken it for test drives two days running. You've put so much mileage on it that either you should buy it for a personal limousine or donate it to the county."

"Great idea!" the driver boomed.

"Don't you think I haven't thought of that already?" Rebecca said testily.

The farther the emergency van took them from the house, the farther Beth realized she was drifting from what was clearly the matter closest to her heart now that her grandmother and great-aunt were out of danger.

Ross.

Chapter Eleven

T he hospital staff seemed amazed that someone as mild-mannered as Jenny Trenton could so easily manage the woman who had terrorized the staff for the past two days. Even though she was technically a patient herself, Aunt Jen took charge. She arranged for the three of them to share a four-bed room, stipulating that the remaining bed be reserved in case another family member joined them before the night was over.

"Louisa," she told Beth and Rebecca. "The poor thing will probably collapse when she's told her husband's been arrested—and why."

Beth was surprised to find herself staying for what remained of the night, but the attending physician convinced her she had a minor concussion and should be kept under observation. Paul had struck her high on the cheek, near the temple. That area was now swollen and throbbing with pain.

Aunt Jen was the only one who took the recommended sedative. Rebecca refused it and Beth followed suit. Thus Beth and her grandmother were left to share the room's false twilight when Aunt Jen began to snore softly. Beth didn't expect Rebecca to speak to her and was surprised when she broke the silence.

"When Paul took you, I thought that was the end of you—the end of the kennels," Rebecca said.

Well, Beth told herself bitterly, *she certainly understands where her priorities lie.* "Arnie can manage the kennels," she told Rebecca. "He can train with me a few months in San Francisco."

"I want *you* to run the kennels. You can get them back to where they were—back on top again—before. . . ."

Rebecca trailed off.

Before you die? Beth glanced at the bed in which her grandmother lay staring at the ceiling. "I can't. I have other responsibilities and commitments."

"Your sister can come live here. This county has—"

Beth cut her off. "My sister isn't baggage to be packed along from job to job. Jenny needs stability and also special programs that—"

It was Rebecca's turn to interrupt. "For a rural area, we have excellent programs for the developmentally disabled. Jen is looking forward to helping the girl with her music."

"She's a grown woman, not a girl," Beth said sternly. It was something she said again and again to apartment managers, salespeople, and well-meaning but wrong-headed neighbors. Then she realized what she had just heard. "Y-you and Aunt Jen talked about bringing my sister here?"

It was a moment before Rebecca responded. Her gruff tone sounded forced. "It was a way to pass the time there in the dark."

Beth's eyes stung. *They intended to take care of Jenny if I died.* Then she realized something else—Rebecca had used the correct term, "developmentally disabled," the larger category to which autistics belonged. That was something most people had to be taught. Rebecca must have investigated Jenny's situation. She also must have looked into the needs of developmentally disabled people, for she mentioned the area's programs for them.

Beth didn't know whether to be happy or angry. For the moment anger was winning out. "What if I didn't 'work out' during these trial weeks? What if I had refused to come here in the first place—or what if I never *existed?* What plans would you have for my sister then?"

"I can tell you one thing!" Rebecca snapped. "No relative of mine will ever end up dependent on the state. Whether or not I ever see *you* again, Jennifer Helen Orne has been well provided for!"

Beth was startled to hear her sister's full name. She saw that only when she had to sign legal documents pertaining to Jenny. Legal documents? Ross had said something about Rebecca changing her will.

Beth saw again Paul Carstairs's eyes, with their methodical coldness. He prided himself in knowing all his mother-in-law's business. Maybe that accounted for why he focused his plan against Jenny. By discrediting her with those letters, maybe he thought he could negate a new will that gave Jenny a portion of what he coveted for himself.

"I don't know," Beth murmured, thinking aloud. "It's not fair to move Jenny into this emotional hornet's nest."

"The guest house could be ready in weeks," Rebecca said, barely hiding her eagerness. "Its parlor would easily accommodate a baby grand for your sister."

"That's still too close to all the bickering, rivalry, and manipulation. I can't take any chances with Jenny's emotional well-being."

"Well, Louisa won't cause any more problems," Rebecca said wearily.

"Louisa isn't the *cause* of any problems I've seen," Beth countered.

Rebecca wasn't listening. "I already decided that if she wants to clear out so badly, let her. Let them all! Let them manage their own money from now on! I wash my hands of it. The trust funds will be generous, but if they can't learn to budget properly for themselves, let them eat cat food until the first of every month! Then they'll begin to understand all I've had to do for them."

Beth sighed. Rebecca was missing the point. Yet if the events of the night had given her enough of a scare to help her decide to release her dependents from their financial apron strings, so much the better for Louisa, Yvonne, Georgia, and Matt. Beth wished Aunt Jen were the one awake instead of Rebecca—or had this been Aunt Jen's intention? To leave the grandmother and her new-found granddaughter "alone" to hash things out?

Just then the hall resounded with the staccato of high heels. Beth recognized the voice accompanying them.

"I *will* see her," Yvonne was insisting, "and you can't stop me. I know my rights!"

The nurse helplessly followed Yvonne into the room and apologized to Rebecca. Beth told the nurse she wanted to take the sedative, after all. She decided she might as well join Aunt Jen and leave Yvonne and Rebecca to lock horns. Why did it have to be Yvonne? Why couldn't it have been Ross who showed up? Where was he?

The sedative went right to work, but not before Beth heard an exchange that amazed her. Yvonne had come to tangle with Rebecca, that was clear. And she certainly was acting as haughty and territorial as ever. But what Beth couldn't believe was the new territory Yvonne had staked out to wrench from Rebecca's grasp—Louisa.

"If you had seen the way those impertinent deputies grilled us at Hollands'—as if *we* were in on Paul's despicable plan!" Yvonne shrilled. "Before they came, we had just begun to talk—much to *your* disappointment, I'm sure. The deputies burst in with their accusations. There sat Louisa, trying to absorb the most *dreadful* news—then to be attacked with questions like that, the two of us! I wouldn't stand for it—I told *them* a thing or two!"

Rebecca asked about Georgia.

"She showed up with Matt just as I was leaving. He'll have to see to her—I'll have my hands full with Louisa. If you think you're going to keep her here dancing to *your* tune, you have another think coming. I've come to tell you that tomorrow I'm taking Louisa to Sacramento where we won't be hounded by reporters. Left alone, she's just witless enough to let them sully the Malvern name. I won't stand for it!"

Drifting toward sleep, Beth couldn't make out Rebecca's next words.

Yvonne's response, however, was clear. "You brought this on yourself. Those forty years living under your thumb made Paul into the creature you saw tonight. I only hope there's still time to introduce Louisa to the values of the side of the family she's been deprived of all these years. I have even higher hopes for Georgia."

Beth drifted into a dream in which Louisa Carstairs turned into a rubbery figure tugged like a rope back and forth between the granite shapes of Rebecca and Yvonne. The most disturbing element of the dream was the way Louisa reacted to being stretched this way and that. For the first time in her life she found herself the center of attention, and clearly she loved it.

Beth woke, caught sight of the ceiling, and shut her eyes again. Wide-open, they made her cheek pulse with pain. Her fingers twitched. She felt immediately that one hand rested inside another, larger hand. Her hand felt warm and secure, as though it had always belonged there.

She didn't need her eyes to tell her whose hand cupped hers. She vaguely remembered that late in the night the hand had found hers, and from that moment on her dreams had stopped their frightening replay of Paul with the gun, Paul stalking her through dark woods.

Nevertheless, she peeked. Ross sat slumped in a chair he had pulled near the bed. He had fallen asleep. The cleft in his chin was dark with stubble. Even darker were the half moons under his eyes.

Not that you look any better just now, she told herself, gingerly touching her cheek with her free hand. The skin was intact but raised and tight with swelling. She could only guess at the color. She squinted around the room. Rebecca was finally asleep like Aunt Jen.

Ross jerked awake.

Beth was trying to think of something clever and cheerful to say, but his sober expression dissuaded her.

"When we found the car like that," he began, "I thought I'd lost you for good."

Beth could hear her heart teaching itself a new tune.

"It made me realize a lot," Ross continued. "I know we haven't known each other long. . . ."

"But we've been through so much in that short time," Beth murmured, hoping she was finishing his thought.

His smile eased some of the weary lines around his eyes. "All I wanted to do last night was to come straight here. But on the walk back to the house, Paul suffered a stroke and I had to stay with him until—"

"Oh, no!" Beth cried. "Was it something I did to him?" She sat up so fast, her head turned into the percussion section of an orchestra.

"Easy," Ross was saying when she dropped from her cloud of pain. "Paul was lucky he had *you* to deal with and not me. He only has himself to blame."

She found herself sitting up fully. Ross had come to her side and was supporting her back. She liked his arm there, solid and warm. She forced herself back to the topic at hand and asked if Paul would recover.

Ross eased onto the bed and sat there, still holding her. "Yes, but to what degree depends on his will to recover. Whether he'll ever be in shape to stand trial is for the courts to decide." He shook his head. "I don't want to talk about Paul."

Beth could have kicked herself for feeling so suddenly shy. "What, then?" was all she could think of to say.

Ross seemed to understand. He struck a lighter tone. "Well, for starters, tell me what you meant when you first saw me—earlier, I mean. A couple of hours ago."

"I don't remember," she said, startled.

He frowned slightly. "I think you were having a nightmare. Maybe you thought the house burned down, after all. You took one look at me and said something odd. 'Bright smoke,' I think it was."

It took a minute for the phrase to hit her. Then Beth

remembered it from the night of her arrival, when she had dreamed about eyes that strange color.

"That bruise practically disappears," Ross was saying, "when you blush. What is it? Are you going to let me in on the secret?"

She glanced at the two other occupied beds. The sisters looked asleep, but with Aunt Jen and her acting, you never knew. "Another time," Beth said. "There are plenty of other things to get straight now that the cat's out of the bag—about who I am, I mean."

Ross was studying her discomfort and looking as though he might laugh at it.

Beth glanced once more at the nearest bed, Rebecca's. Even asleep, Rebecca's presence was dampening. Beth sighed to herself and decided this wasn't the time to come across as anything but breezy or businesslike. "Now that I've turned out to be in the family," she resumed, "I guess that officially makes you and me some kind of cousins."

She saw mischief, then something else, catch flame in those eyes of bright smoke.

"Even if my father hadn't been adopted," Ross began, "this is the *only* kind of cousins I would ever consider us." He drew her closer. "Kissing cousins."

He was gentle, careful not to touch her sore cheek when he first kissed her. By the second one, Beth had forgotten all about that cheek. And even Aunt Jen's muffled chuckles faded into happy oblivion by the time Beth lost herself in a third kiss.